W9-CCP-215

The True Tale of Sleeping Beauty

PHILOMEL BOOKS
A division of Penguin Young Readers Group.
Published by The Penguin Group.
Penguin Group (USA) Inc., 375 Hudson Street, New York, NY 10014, U.S.A.
Penguin Group (Canada), 90 Eglinton Avenue East, Suite 700, Toronto,
Ontario M4P 2Y3, Canada (a division of Pearson Penguin Canada Inc.).
Penguin Books Ltd, 80 Strand, London WC2R 0RL, England.
Penguin Ireland, 25 St. Stephen's Green,
Dublin 2, Ireland (a division of Penguin Books Ltd).
Penguin Group (Australia), 250 Camberwell Road, Camberwell,
Victoria 3124, Australia (a division of Pearson Australia Group Pty Ltd).
Penguin Books India Pvt Ltd, 11 Community Centre,
Panchsheel Park, New Delhi—110 017, India.
Penguin Group (NZ), 67 Apollo Drive, Rosedale, Auckland 0632,
New Zealand (a division of Pearson New Zealand Ltd).
Penguin Books (South Africa) (Pty) Ltd, 24 Sturdee Avenue,
Rosebank, Johannesburg 2196, South Africa.
Penguin Books Ltd, Registered Offices: 80 Strand, London WC2R 0RL, England.

 Published simultaneously in Canada.
Printed in the United States of America.

Edited by Jill Santopolo. Design by Amy Wu. Text set in 11.5 point Adobe Caslon.

Library of Congress Cataloging-in-Publication Data
Yolen, Jane. Curse of the thirteenth fey / Jane Yolen. p. cm.
Summary: Accident-prone, thirteen-year-old Gorse, the youngest fairy
in her family, falls into a trap while on her way to the palace to bless the
newborn princess, Talia, but arrives in time to give a gift which,
although seemingly horrific, may prove to be a real blessing in this
take-off on the classic tale of Sleeping Beauty.
[1. Fairy tales. 2. Fairies—Fiction. 3. Magic—Fiction. 4. Elves—Fiction.
5. Family life—Fiction. 6. Prophecies—Fiction.]
I. Title. PZ8.Y78Th 2012 [Fic]—dc23 2011038847

ISBN 978-0-399-25664-6
1 3 5 7 9 10 8 6 4 2

Curse OF THE Thirteenth Fey

The True Tale of Sleeping Beauty

JANE YOLEN

PHILOMEL BOOKS
An Imprint of Penguin Group (USA) Inc.

ALSO BY THE SAME AUTHOR:

Snow in Summer

Girl in a Cage

The Devil's Arithmetic

Queen's Own Fool

For those Fey friends in Scotland:
Deborah Turner Harris, Bob Harris, Elizabeth Wein,
Elizabeth Kerner, Lisa Tuttle—never seen enough,
but your e-mails, postings, friendships keep me writing.

Also for editor Jill Santopolo and my daughter
Heidi Stemple, who keep me honest. For Debby Harris,
beta reader extraordinaire. For Marcel Sislowitz,
who did the plot dance around the tribal fire and shook
some gourds at the sky for me, as well as offering me
guano. For Adam Stemple, who suggested how the guano
might be used. And for my Facebook friends, especially
Steven Beard, Kevin Andrew Murphy, Tanja Wooten,
and Geoffrey A. Landis, who helped
make things go *Boom!*

An earlier version of this story was published as a short story called "The Thirteenth Fey" © 1985 in *Dragonfield and Other Stories*. For those interested in more about the Shouting Fey, two other short stories have been published: "The Uncorking of Uncle Finn" (© 1986, in *F&SF* magazine and reprinted in two of my collections, *Storyteller* and *Sister Emily's Lightship*) and "Dusty Loves" (© 1988, *F&SF* magazine and also reprinted in *Sister Emily's Lightship*).

TO THE READER OF THIS BOOK

These are the names
of the Shouting Fey in this story
and in Gorse's life.
Speak of them with respect,
for they can become your best friends
or your worst enemies.
Never, ever challenge them
to a Shout Off, for you will lose—
your hair, your voice, your home,
and possibly your life.
You have been warned.

•THE SHOUTING FEY•

Great-grandfather **Fergus**, long dead.

Great-grandmother **Banshee,** Fergus's wife, long dead.

Great-great-aunt **Loireg**, patroness of Hebridean spinners and spinsters, long dead.

Great-aunts **Gemma** and **Gerne** (Gorse's Grandmother), long dead.

Great-aunt **Gilda**, the only Great still alive, the Family's healer, who never had children.

The Aunts, children of Fergus and Banshee: **Galda**, **Glade**, **Granne**, **Grania**, **Gardenia**, **Goldie**, and **Mother**, the seventh daughter.

•THE COUSINS•

Alliford, he of the twisted toes and bright red hair, much of a weeper.

Cousin **Mallow**, whey-faced and whiny.

Cousin **Maribel**, who refused to pull any bow, soon to declare for vegetarianism.

And seven other unnamed others, three boys and four girls.

•GORSE'S IMMEDIATE FAMILY•

Father, of Irish elven ancestry.

Mother, whose birth name was Grete.

•THE THIRTEEN ELVEN-FEY CHILDREN•

(seven girls, six boys)

1. **Necrops**: firstborn son,
noble of bearing, boisterous and burning.

2. **Darna**: firstborn daughter,
works hard, and all with a certain elegance.

3. **Carnell**: brother,
does silly walks and silly talks
but has a strong right hand.

4. **Willow**: sister,
sexy and secretive at the same time.

5. **Thorn**: sister,
as prickly as her namesake.

6. **Arian**: brother,
a bit slow but with the sweetest smile.

7. **Solange**: the beauty,
seventh child of a seventh child.

8. **Bobbin**: eldest
of the twin boys by a minute.

9. **Robbin**: youngest
of the twin boys by a minute.

10. **Cambria**: sister,
pert, sometimes to the point of silliness.

11. **Aster**: sister,
Great-aunt Gilda's favorite and most like her.

12. **Dusty**: brother,
the Romeo of the Shouting Fey and Gorse's best friend.

13. **Gorse**: the youngest,
who tells this story, later Keeper of Books.

Part I

A SPELL AGAINST AGUE

Fever, favor someone else,

Let peace be mine this day.

Leave my child, remove yourself,

For she is just a little Fey.

Take away the chills and sweats,

The vivid dreams that shake her sleep.

Leave my child, remove yourself,

Or I will give you cause to weep.

Out, out, damned fever,

Leave her! Leave her!

·1·

THE FAMILY

In the middle of a stand of white birch sits a decaying pavilion. The white columns have been pocked by generations of our peashooters. Several kite strings, quite stained by the local birds, still twine around the capitals. The kites themselves are long gone, torn off and taken by the weather imps to line their own drafty halls.

In late spring, west winds whistle through the thin pavilion walls. The rains—quite heavy in November and April—have left runnels in the wallpaper that look like patterns one should be able to identify and never quite can. It's very old wallpaper anyway. As a child I used to see different pictures there after every rain.

But I would change nothing about the house. Nothing about the birch trees. Nothing about the small hill on which the pavilion stands.

This perfect place is familiar. It is family. It is where I want to be and nowhere else.

It is home.

"A girl!" Great-aunt Gilda cried, for once modulating her voice. "The thirteenth fey."

"That's important," Aunt Galda added, as if she alone could have known. "Thirteenth."

"*The* thirteenth!" Aunts Grania and Glade repeated, lest no one miss the fact.

Mother sighed, with exhaustion, with hope. "Maybe she's—"

"No maybe about it." Great-aunt Gilda's voice was always certain, even in modulation. "She's the thirteenth. Are you unable to count your own children, Grete?"

"I was going to say *maybe* she's the One."

"I meant that, too." Great-aunt Gilda's voice was rising. Nobody wanted that, not there, with a vulnerable newborn who'd only cried once.

The other Aunts quickly cleaned me up and wrapped me in a gown, the long lacy naming gown each of the children had worn in turn. I began another cry, this one high and cranky, a complaint about the light or the Aunts' loud voices, or maybe it was hunger or anger or fear. But once tightly wrapped, my limbs stilled, I lay quiet, as if bespelled. The Aunts, too, said nothing more. In that small quietness, Mother named me, quickly, before anyone else had a chance to.

"Gorse," she said.

The Aunts all looked appalled, their faces pinched.

"Hardly euphonious," said Aunt Glade, always a stickler for proper sounds. "It rhymes with *coarse* and *horse*. I don't dare imagine the spells."

"Gorse," Mother said again.

"Are you *sure*?" Aunt Gardenia asked. "Gorse is such a weed, and I am always pulling it up out of the flower beds. Besides, it's prickly."

"Gorse!" Mother said firmly, and—as it was the third time—the magick held. "She'll need to be as hardy as a weed, to make her way through twelve brothers and sisters, not to mention the cousins. And the Aunts." She drew a deep breath. "Besides, I like the sunny yellow flowers."

"It's a *weed*," Aunt Gardenia grumbled again, but the other Aunts overruled her.

"Hardy it is, then," they agreed, and went off to make a spell for me.

Along the way, they got distracted by my brother Dusty

falling out of the tree house, where he was much too young to have been taken without yet knowing how to use his wings to break his fall.

At the very same moment, my sister Solange had said a Curse, though as she was considered a child, not yet sixteen, it could still be reversed, but that had to be done before it could set.

So half of the Aunts went to reverse the spell and half to mend whatever might have been broken by Dusty's fall, which turned out to be only his pride, or as much pride as a two-year-old has. The hardiness the Aunts were going to confer on me got delayed, and by the time they got back, I was already whatever I was going to be anyway, and so I spent a childhood in and out of fevers and headaches and agues of one kind or another, some brought about by an allergy to different kinds of magick, some by sitting in damp places. But I was hardy in all other ways.

Or at least that's the story they told me years later. Like all fey stories, this one has grown in the telling. We in the Family all do that: we make Family stories better. Better than they are, better than they were, better than the truth. After a while, the story *becomes* the truth because no one actually remembers how things really happened.

The one true thing I know about my birth is that I was born in my parents' pavilion, on the same marble and velvet couch they'd used for the lying-in of each of my brothers and sisters. We ate, slept, argued, and played in that pavilion, under wall plaques emblazoned with Family mottoes. *Curses begin with lies* ran one. *Spells begin with the truth* was another. The pair hung on either side of the big fireplace. *Every Oath leads to the stars* was a third; it was hanging in the kitchen. A fourth—*Bad thoughts warp magick*—was in Father's library, over a collection of books about ogres and trolls. And above my bed, along with a list of my siblings, beginning with number one, Necrops, and ending with me, number thirteen, Gorse, hung a plaque that said simply *Be careful around magick.*

Like my siblings, I spent hours strapped to my baby board in the lower branches of the birch trees. There I was watched over by butterflies, dragonflies, and of course ladybugs that sat on my nose and made me sneeze. The mourning doves sang me to sleep with their soft *coo-coo-roo*s. A murder of crows woke me each morning with their shrieks.

Father told me about all that, and—unlike the fey—elves do not lie. It is an old Curse set upon them, so old that even Father, who knows *everything,* does not know how and when it was laid. Sometimes elvish truth telling is so harsh, one would wish they could couch it more softly the way we fey do—in story or fib or fabulation. But elves simply cannot tell an untruth.

We thirteen children of Mother and Father are an odd

mix, truth and lies coming alternately from our mouths, sometimes at the same moment, sometimes months and years apart, and even we don't always know the difference.

Like most faerie childhoods, mine included much that was beautiful, with only the occasional night fright. The woods, the sky, the trees, the creatures, the wind through my wings, the murmuration of the nearby brook . . . what could be better than that?

Yet it was all to come to an end one fateful day, or at least an end to what the Family knew best, though it was a long, slow unwinding to get us to that day. Much as we had hoped for that ending, we fey don't like or understand change. But even for us, as long-lived as we are, change is inevitable. Spring becomes summer, summer becomes fall, and even the fey finally grow old.

The Family was awash with cousins and Aunts, though Uncles were in short supply. They tended to stay only for a short while and then disappear, heading back to the human world, which was where they belonged. Off they'd go through the part of the woods we called the Wooing Path. Though it was the straightest route to the castle, we fey were forbidden to travel it, though occasionally, when he was older, Dusty liked to fly high above it. He always had a wild streak in him. That can make a scoundrel or a hero, and which he would become was always a topic of conversation among the Aunts until the very end of this story.

That the Uncles disappeared after a year or two didn't seem to matter to the Aunts, who had the babies they'd always wanted, which was the usual Shouting Fey way, since marriageable male fey were in short supply.

"I'm afraid most of you will have to make do with humans," was the way Great-aunt Gilda put it. "We did."

Not Mother. She'd chosen Father in a contest of some sort, and the prize had been the actual marriage. The Aunts, though, believed Mother had married beneath her, and they weren't slow in letting Father know how they felt about him being only an elf, and an Irish one at that, and therefore not a full fey.

"Elf-knot," Great-aunt Gilda often called him witheringly.

The Aunts bantered with names for his ears, like "Elephant Man." Aunt Galda even said, "You could learn to fly with those ears," which meant she was pointing to his winglessness as well. Faeries have gorgeous wings, some batlike with flexible pinions, and some with dragonfly wings as veined as cathedral windows. But elves—well, they don't have wings at all.

But Father never responded in kind to the taunts from the Family, retreating instead to his library, which was stocked with books of the past, present, and future, the only library of its kind in the known universe. That library was both a place of study and a refuge for him.

And for me.

Father had long collected books through a small hole in the wall of the pavilion, which only he'd discovered and only he seemed to be able to work. He would reach in, feel around, then say, "Got you!" and pull out a volume, never knowing what he would get. It was a hole, after all, not a window, and he daren't stick a candle or lantern down there for fear of setting the rest of the books on fire, wherever they were.

The dates on the books Father found were so varied, he eventually came to understand that he was reaching into different times and climes, different libraries or bookshops around the known and unknown world. Slowly—because he could not retrieve a book every time he tried—he built up quite a collection and began putting it in order. In fact, ordering that library became his life's work. He was the first Keeper of Books the Family had ever had.

That is how Father became extremely well read in Gramarye, of course, but also Astrology, Astronomy, Archaeology, Architecture—"the important *A*'s," he called them. He also knew Philosophy, History, Mineralogy, Necrology—and Computer Science, an art whose time was yet to come. The Aunts didn't read—though they *could*—preferring instead to tell stories and embroider taradiddles, gossip, and lies.

Mother? Well, Mother was always a puzzle to me. She didn't defend Father, but she didn't condemn him either. Until . . . well, that comes rather further along in the story.

Besides his large, pointed ears, Father also had a strong nose, rather like a hawk's beak, and the bluest eyes. His was the gentlest soul in the Family, if somewhat shy on magick. His elven ancestry showed most prominently in those ears, which he was careful to hide under a fringe of graying hair so as not to plague the Aunts. His lack of wings he disguised beneath loose jackets, the pockets of which were always stuffed with sweets for all the Family's children. He always carried a book with him, sometimes more than one.

I never heard him raise his voice.

The Aunts *could* have left Father alone. They dwelt nearby in their own decaying whimsies, reposes, follies, and belvederes; close enough for picnics, far enough away for secrets. But almost as if Father's mere presence was an insult—or perhaps they thought it was his fault that we were no longer a Family Under the Hill, though that had happened in the Great-greats' time, so he certainly couldn't be blamed for that—the Aunts continued to sniff at him.

Believe me, they were very accomplished sniffers. It would take a lot for them to forgive him.

Father didn't return their sniffs, or even act as if he'd heard them. And Mother, her beautiful face serene, not a bit of her golden hair, caught up in its gilded hairnet, disturbed, seemed not to notice them either, which was just as well, since she was never so gentle as Father. After all, we were of the line of the Shouting Fey, who can cause death and consternation simply by the timbre of our voices.

Yes, we were Shouters, born and trained, though amongst ourselves we were known as the Family. To all others, we were the Shouting Fey.

How does that work? It is our magick, the little that is left us. That and the few implements of the Old Magick, things like wands, spindles, a long piece of the thread of life, all things that were light enough to carry and could be hastily packed up.

According to Great-aunt Gilda, when we came into the human world, much of what the fey can do—the vast array of wishes, enchantments, large glamours—was stripped away from us by the vengeful Unseelie faerie court. And if you are on the run, who could carry a large Vanishing Cupboard or Renewal Chamber? Or perhaps the magick was simply leached out of us by living so long close to humans.

Great-aunt Gilda tells the story both ways, depending upon her mood, her humors, if it is raining, or if it's a Tuesday. When she is in a remembering mood, she reminds us how it was back when we lived Under the Hill, when glamours and the Renewal Chamber would have kept her young and beautiful, without the need for an entire table of useless powders and paints. She would always add with a heavy sigh, "Those were the days when our world was as full of wishes as the sea is filled with fishes." Though of course she was born here and not Under the Hill and only had the stories from her Mother and Father, who died before she reached her majority.

It has always been Father's hope to try and find out through his books what is missing and perhaps get it all back. But none of the Aunts understands that. Or if they did once, they no longer do. Instead, they rely on the Shout, that one big piece of magick that has remained with the Family, though a Minor Shout can only be done once a day at most. As for a Major Shout, it may take up to a week for the Shouter to recover. Great Magicks are like that. You expend all your magickal energy and are left in a state of near coma, like me in a fever. Besides, it takes years and lots of study before any of us can be good enough to control a Shout. I am still trying. Or as Dusty likes to say, "Goosey—you are *very* trying."

Now, Great-aunt Gilda can bring down milk from dried-up cows with one voice or gum it up with another. Aunt Glade can curdle blood in the veins of man or beast with a low growl. Aunt Goldie's Shout drops horses in the meadow, and that can be a good thing in battle, but it's something else altogether when it's a farmer's large herd on his own land, which occasionally grazes too near us. Aunt Grania is able to scream in six registers at once. As a child she broke windows in all of the Western Counties when a silly prince Bid her do it for a lark.

Over the years, the women of our court have honed their Shouts: Aunt Glade has a voice that can startle starlings from their nests. Aunt Gardenia can shout down rooftops, scattering the pantiles in four different directions when she *really* gets going. Aunt Goldie has been known to lift the wigs off the heads of human judges in the middle of their deliberations with a single loud hum. And Mother's Shout is said to cause the dead to rise and the lame to dance. She's a seventh child, after all.

To be truthful, I've never actually seen any of those dread things happen with a Shout. Not by any of them. But of course I've heard all the stories. As for Mother, I knew she could lift a slow-moving child fifteen steps away from danger simply by the power of her voice. This is exactly what happened to me one soft summer night at a family picnic.

I'd fallen asleep and was sleepwalking, heading toward a cliff, when she found me and Shouted me back.

Oh, the women of the Family have many varieties of Shouts, but in my opinion, Mother's cliff-rescuer was the very best. Until . . . well, you shall hear about that anon.

Now, this story *really* begins with a Royal Bidding, and Royal Biddings always start the same way. Some idiotic prince or princess or other member of the royal family demands a charm or a favor, and we must respond. We cannot do otherwise. It has been laid upon us as if it's a Curse, and it's my opinion it certainly is.

Sometimes in a Bidding things work out for everyone.

Perhaps the girl the prince desires is persuaded by a charm to love him in return.

Perhaps a king's war is won by a Shout.

Perhaps a prince's enemy is changed into a toad.

Perhaps a queen gets a baby by means of a Wish.

But often the Biddings go awfully, terribly wrong. A beautiful girl is changed into a horror by a jealous princess because a fey was Bidden to do it. A bishop is struck by lightning because a duke covets his land. A young boy is crippled because a princeling wants to win a race.

We Shouting Fey have to do as we are Bidden. We cannot question the royal who asks. And we are Forbidden, I don't know how, to use magick for or against a royal unless we are specifically asked. It takes cunning and charm to work around Biddings, which is why we children are not supposed to talk to the royals about them. Mother said it was because we didn't know enough, but Father disagreed. "You children are too transparent," he said, by which he meant we lied badly. And of course he never lied at all.

One Bidding I remember in particular began when a squire sent by Lady Caledon came wheedling up to Aunt Goldie's front door. She wasn't home, but my brothers Necrops and Dusty and two of our cousins were playing in front of her whimsy with a golden ball they'd found in a well. They hadn't known it belonged to anyone, and certainly not to Lady Caledon.

When the squire started his long, whiny run-up to the actual Bidding, Necrops—too loudly and almost in a full Shout—said, "Get on with it, already. You're ruining our game." Boys take games very seriously. And, after all, the squire was hardly royal, just a lackey sent by a lady.

The almost Shout blew the squire all the way back to Lady Caledon's small house. She complained at once to the king, who was *not* amused. He sent two of his men-at-arms to bring a large iron bar to set against Aunt Goldie's front door, knowing that none of us fey could move the bar. We're terribly allergic to iron. In the worst case, it can cause the True Death.

Poor Aunt Goldie looked out of her window in dismay. She was much too old and much too fat to go climbing out the window, and her whimsy had no back door.

Brave Necrops knew it was his fault, so he went to move the thing and rescue Aunt Goldie from her confinement. He'd actually managed to pick up one end of the bar before screaming and dropping it, and breaking out in spots from head to toe. Well, I never actually saw all the spots, but Father said it was so, so it had to be true.

The cousins ran off. They usually do when things get hot. But young as he was, Dusty went over to examine the bar, put his hand on it, and was burned. He still has the scar to this day. Still, he didn't let that burn stop him. He squatted there for nearly an hour, drawing plans in the dirt with his finger till he figured out that, with a tree limb as a lever, he could move the bar a little, though it was so heavy it had taken two men-at-arms to carry it. And once he'd shifted the bar, he was able to send it rolling along with a small Shout until it had gathered enough momentum to roll down a hill on its own, fetching up against a tree along the Wooing Path.

After that, he was a hero in Aunt Goldie's eyes, even when he was a scamp to all the others.

Unusually, Father gave the boys a tongue-lashing, then handed Dusty a book on levers and fulcrums by someone called Archimedes, and returned the golden ball to Lady Caledon with a note regretting his eldest son's behavior.

"The note hurt me not at all," Father said, "and may have stopped further Biddings from that quarter. And it wasn't a lie because I did regret greatly that the boys' behavior caused themselves and your Aunt Goldie such pain." He was right, of course. Lady Caledon never Bid any of us to do anything again, as she married out of our kingdom and was gone from us forever.

So, now you know all about Shouts and Biddings. But you need to understand one more thing before I tell you the whole story.

From our earliest walking days, we children of the Family played together in the fields and meadows and woods around our houses, though not along the Wooing Path, of course. The games we played were simple ones, like Red Rover, Fly Over, or Beggar My Lady, like Which Flower of Power Are You, as well as the ever-popular Tag. While we girls played with cornstalk dolls, ivy-plaited jump ropes, and pretend stoves that could almost but not quite warm up river water with our feeble heating spells, the boys all played mumblety-peg with wooden knives carved from the bole of a lightning-split sycamore. They dared one another to fly the highest or the fastest. They bet acorns and apples on the outcome.

One time Dusty challenged Carnell to a boxing match,

and we all watched as Carnell knocked him out with a single right hook. When Dusty woke, Necrops had Carnell in a grip around his neck.

"Swear," Necrops said angrily. "Take an Oath that you'll never hit anyone younger or smaller again." His arm tightened around Carnell's neck until Carnell was ready to swear.

Just then, Father—who'd been alerted by the noise—came outside and heard the last bit.

"Let him go. Let him go *now*!" His voice was sharper than I'd ever heard before. "If he had spoken that Oath, here where there is still a magick surround, and then if by accident or design, he violated that Oath, he would burst into a thousand stars. Do you, Necrops, want to be responsible for your brother's death?" Father's voice ended on a ragged note, the word *death* seemingly enough to scare him as well.

Necrops looked shaken; Carnell even more so. They hugged each other and then together helped Dusty stand. Then all the boys went over to Grandfather Oak, where the grand tree house sat in its long branches. They climbed up quickly, and Mother sent up a pot of dandelion tea and a platter of rough cheese toasties.

We girls weren't invited, of course. We were never allowed into the tree house. That didn't stop us getting in, of course. We could still work minor mirages and glamours, so we could always disguise ourselves as one of the boys. And unless that particular boy was in the tree house at the time, we were not discovered.

That same day, Solange glamoured herself and—looking just like Cousin Alliford, from his twisted toes to his bright red hair—she flew to the top of the tree. Slowly she shinnied down the trunk. What she didn't know was that as she was climbing down, Alliford was climbing up. They both got to the tree-house door at the exact same moment.

Push and pull, pull and push.

Alliford was no match for a seventh child of a seventh child, and he tumbled down, hitting branch after branch along the way. There was a tear in the primary of his left wing—he had dragonfly wings, and they tear quite easily. He hurried back to Great-aunt Gilda for a weep (he was always a weeper), a bit of healing, and some sassafras tea.

Meanwhile, Solange, glamour intact, went into the tree house for the tea and toasties, and got to smoke forbidden hazel squibs with the boys and try her hand at mumblety-peg. She was much better than Alliford at tossing the knife, which made the boys a bit suspicious, but she waved them off, saying, "I've been practicing."

As for the hazel squibs, they made her sick, of course.

Girls simply can't do that without throwing up. But as she told us afterward, "Every bit of puke was worth it."

But that was the day I learned about the power of Oaths and about the starbursts. And while then it seemed like a romantic notion of death, when it came to it, I realized that Dead is Dead and awfully final. Not romantic at all.

·2·

SHOUTING FEY

Mother thought I was blessed with the Sight, something every fey family looks for in a child, and especially, as it turned out, the Shouting Fey. It was because each time I had the ague—and I was often sick—I had wild dreams.

"The Sight comes once in every third generation," Mother announced at an all-Family picnic, the first time I'd ever heard of any such thing. I'd had another bad night of fever dreams, and she was telling the Aunts all about it.

I was almost four, sitting in her lap, and lisped in a childish voice, "What's the Sight?"

"A hope, a wish . . . ," she said, stroking my straight, dark hair. I was the only one who was dark, the only one who looked like Father. The others all had milkweed fluff, white-gold and flyway curls. True fey hair.

"Not just a hope and a wish. A necessity," Great-aunt Gilda added.

By Mother's side, Father was dishing out the mallow and marmalade sandwiches, silently. He loved his children as we were, not for what we might be. What he lacked in the ability to fly, he more than made up in patience and love, *not* a family trait of the Shouting Fey. We tend to be competitive and say what we think.

Later at the picnic, Solange told me that the Aunts had mentioned the possibility that I might be the One, and she didn't say it pleasantly.

"They're *looking* at you," she said, pointing a finger at me that might as well have been a poisoned arrow. "Because you are the thirteenth, and no one guessed you were coming. Because you have wild dreams. Because you flew early. Because . . . well, because. Don't expect anything to come of it." She glared over at the Aunts, then turned back and said, "They looked at me, too, because I'm the seventh and the only one born with a caul." She meant a veil of skin, which is supposed to be magickal. Evidently nothing had come of them looking at *her*. I thought she was just jealous.

"What's *expect*?" I asked.

"Wanting something to be true when it isn't," she said.

"I expect honey cake." I looked longingly at the golden brown cake sitting on the blanket next to the big withy basket.

Solange huffed through her nose and turned her back on me. She already had the Aunts' sniff down and was working on her own version of the Shout. I'd eavesdropped on her practicing out in the meadow using a voice that was both angry and loud. Butterflies had fallen in little patches and shreds from the trees as a result. It was impressive and sad at the same time. I carried a pocketful of the dead butterflies back to Father, hoping he could reanimate them, but when I drew them out of my pocket, there was nothing left but dust.

However, my expectation of that honey cake was quickly satisfied by Father, who cut the cake and offered me the very first slice. So, I thought no more of my failure to be "the One." At not yet four, my expectations were small and easily filled.

Yet, I *had* been marked by being the thirteenth child. And as Solange had said, there'd been other signs as well. I'd been early to walk, even earlier to talk. And when I flew by myself at two, long before anyone even realized my tiny wings were fully opened, Mother was *positive* I was the fey spoken of in the prophecy, though prophecies are notably hard to read and usually only understood long after they've been fulfilled. Still, that never stopped any Shouting Fey from trying to figure one out.

The prophecy about the One ran like this:

The One comes into the daylight veiled,
So long awaited, hoped for, hailed
Where others tried and always failed.
And from a deep and darkened space,
A Savior of an ancient race,
The One will, wingless, come apace.
With brand-new wings, the One can fly,
Makes truth come out of ancient lie,
So severs bonds and every tie.

No one knew what "veiled" meant, or which lie was referred to, or indeed what ancient race was meant, but when I flew early, all the Aunts and Mother were convinced I was the One.

My first flight was not a real flight, of course. I merely hopped, skipped, and lifted above the ground for about twelve seconds, covering a distance of no more than seventeen feet, most of it downhill. I screamed all the way, more with delight than fear. As it was a scream and not a Shout, I only distracted the bluebirds and crows without disturbing so much as a feather. Lucky for them.

Darna was supposed to be looking after me, and she took her duties seriously, so she ran to tell the others. That left me to tumble down the rest of the muddy hill unwatched. It was the beginning of my role as the accident-prone one of the Family. The number thirteen at work, I suppose. I hit my head on a small protruding rock and lay unresponsive for almost a minute before Darna came back with Mother and the Aunts.

When they found me at the bottom of the hill, a bit mixed up from the head bump, there was confusion and distress. They fluttered their hands (Solange told me this) but were careful not to Shout. Father was summoned from the library, but I woke up before he arrived. For a moment, my eyes crossed and I couldn't focus properly.

I touched my mouth with a muddy hand, saying, "Please, some milk, Mistress Bossy." I was incredibly thirsty and, for some reason, thought my kin were cows, the lovely black-and-white kind.

This strained things for a few minutes till Mother realized I wasn't being sassy but merely concussed. At that, they hastily gathered me up, cured my bruises with their healing touches, and argued about whether I had the Sight or not.

"Certainly she has Flight," said Great-aunt Gilda.

"That doesn't mean she has Sight," Aunt Glade pointed out.

"Different first letters means a different spell," Aunt Granne added, always turning the obvious into the mysterious.

Me, I fell asleep during their long concatenation that went from Flight to Height to Blight to Sight and back again. According to Father, who was studying about it, the Shouting Fey are the only ones who still hold to rhyme in their spells. At least according to his books.

"If it was good enough for the ancestors . . ." Great-aunt Gilda intoned as always.

At this point Father arrived, scooped me up in his arms, and took me back to the library, where I spent a lovely afternoon on the couch, a blanket lapped over me and whatever books I wanted read to me on a table by my side. In between naps, I heard every single one of them twice. Father had a lovely reading voice: lilting, mellow, and convincing.

As Solange had said, there were also my vivid dreams that convinced the Aunts I was the One. In those dreams I seemed to see a strange future, where humans flew through the air on iron wings, babies were born in bottles, and food was plucked from boxes filled with winter ice and light.

It turned out those dreams were sent to me by any ague

or earache that I came down with, or by the peculiar swirling patterns of the moldy wallpaper in my bedroom, or from an unidentified allergy to flyspeck not diagnosed until I was a grown-up.

Besides, the dreams were odd conversions of the things I'd read about in the library. No one truly understood this. Except for Father, none of the Aunts read much, and my siblings didn't read at all.

I was, in my Father's words, "ever a surprise."

At each dream, the Aunts gathered again, standing over my cot, my bed, my library chair, my bale of hay, wherever I was couched at the time. They listened to my maunderings, then they wrangled about the meanings, made charts, laid on hands, tried to figure out what my prophesies meant. As they'd done that day at the family picnic.

The one who almost always sat by me with a cool compress or warm milk, rocking me through the worst of my dreams, was Father and, occasionally, my brother Dusty. Dusty often brought a little gift, usually something sparkly he'd found somewhere. His nickname in the Family was Mr. Magpie, and the shelves of his room were stuffed with bits he found all over the place—glittering globes, silver ribbons, shining buttons or coins, bits of broken glass, and rocks with sparkly stuff in them.

Hardly anyone else ever sat with me as I battled through

a fever. They all seemed to feel that if a thing couldn't be solved by magickal healing, it wasn't worth solving.

Father took a much more practical approach. "You'll be fine," he'd say, mixing honey in the milk. "Nothing to worry about," he'd promise, wringing out another cool cloth for my head. "Close your eyes, and I'll read to you," he'd tell me, and he always did.

I expected his calm, quiet presence at my sickbed, and if he couldn't be there, and someone else besides Dusty sat with me instead, I'd make myself sicker with my weeping and demands until whoever was caring for me found Father in the library and he came running to my side, storybook in hand.

As the years went by, it became clear to the Aunts that none of my childish predictions had come true. So they stopped asking me to look into the future, realizing that I was simply guessing. Or inventing. Or borrowing from the books I'd read. What humans call "storying" when they do it themselves. Or when someone else does it, they call it "telling a lie."

"Not that imagination is to be sniffed at," said Aunt Glade one afternoon, leaning over my sickbed. Her wattle shook as she spoke. Then she sniffed loudly. I didn't miss the irony of that sniff, but I didn't move a muscle.

As Aunt Glade turned away, her voluminous skirt swishing like leaves skittering over a human road, I heard her mutter to Mother, "That's what comes from mixing with elves. You get weak children." She sniffed again, though softer this time, and added, "You married him for naught."

Mother said nothing in return. *Nothing.*

They both believed I was asleep, but truly I wasn't. As I often did, I was only pretending to sleep. That way I could listen in on the grown-ups' conversations. By six, I'd become a professional eavesdropper. It was the only way to learn anything in the Family. For all they were great Shouters, the Aunts and Mothers were also great keepers of secrets. Of course the problem with listening in when others think you are sleeping is that sometimes you hear something you wished you hadn't.

What I heard that day seemed so awful that I almost sat up and screamed at the two of them. Screaming is not Shouting. There are rules for Shouts, and only lungs and bad temper for screams. At six, I had a child's version of the Shout and thought I'd dimmed the stars one evening when I was out practicing in my secret meadow, which lay on the other side of a copse of trees from the Wooing Path. Probably I'd simply mistaken a bank of clouds for my own work. As frightened as I was then of what *might* have been my power, part of me was sure I'd never have enough. After all, I was more elf than fey, and elves have no ability to Shout at all. But instead of sitting up and asking what Aunt Glade meant, or why Mother didn't just Shout her down, I lay there, tears pooling beneath closed lids, my heart broken. I could feel the jagged pieces in my chest.

It didn't matter that Aunt Glade thought me weak. Clearly I was. No one else in the Family was sick in bed at least twice a season, and sometimes more. No one else ran fevers like mine. No one else got sick headaches whenever too much magick was present.

No, that wasn't what made me ready to scream myself hoarse. It was the other words—"You married him for naught"—that raced about in my head. Had Mother only married Father to get a man to stay around for the Family? For the first time, I'd overheard a secret I didn't want to know. I suddenly understood something that should never have been mine to understand. Mother didn't love Father, had *never* loved him, had used him for whatever wicked purposes the women of the Shouting Fey use their men. No wonder the human Uncles kept disappearing. Who would want to stay if he was unloved, unwanted, uncared for?

I convinced myself in the middle of my hysteria that probably now Mother and Father would be separated, what we fey called a "dissolvement," and Father—like the

Uncles—would disappear from our lives forever. Perhaps he'd wander off a high cliff in despair, not having wings like a fey to fly down gracefully. I imagined him dead fifty ways before I fell into a real fever sleep brought about by sadness and fear, where I dreamed even more disasters, earthquakes, conspiracies, and the Great War, all things I'd read about and only half understood.

A BRIEF EXPLANATION OF THE FEY, WHICH FATHER TOLD ME ONE NIGHT

In the old country of the Fey, which lay Under the Hill, there were counties larger than any human regions, states, or shires. And that country was divided into two great faerie courts.

The Seelie Court was where the good faeries congregated, though "good" in the old tongue merely meant blessed, or lucky. There were many—both human and fey—who saw nothing good about the Seelie folk at all. Father said the Seelie folk talked about doing good, wrote ballads about it, yet never actually helped anyone but themselves . . . to their neighbors' property, jewels, and spells.

The Unseelie Court was where the reputed bad faeries danced the night away, or at least they danced when they were not off playing tricks on humans like stealing their children or leading them into poison ivy while the humans thought they were in a faerie grotto, or leaving boogers on the Seelie Queen's crown that looked like precious jewels until dawn. When Father talked about them, he spoke in hushed tones. "No need to alert them," he said, only naming them in whispers.

"Why, Father?" I asked. "Will they hurt us?"

"They will try," he said, "because they are cold, distant, cruel, and unfeeling." Then he saw me shudder, so he added quickly, "But Mother and the Aunts will keep us safe."

I thought there was little to choose between the two courts, and said so.

Father had laughed, that water-over-stones laugh of his. Cupping my chin in his right hand, he told me, "You are too wise for your years, but remember this: stealing your jewels and stealing your soul are leagues apart. However, I don't want you to even think *about wandering Under the Hill, child. Better to stay up here in the Light, where the wind puzzles through the trees, fish leap in our streams, and we can follow the running of the deer . . ." He looked away to the far hills, to the West, where his own people lived. Or where his people once lived.* We're *his own people now.*

And then I thought about the third court, our court, the Court of the Shouting Fey. We don't live Under the Hill but above it. In the soft air. In the green meadows. Father said that according to Great-aunt Gilda, the Under the Hill folk consider us a silly, useless, powerless few. They call us "the Misfits" or "the Losers" and sometimes "the Quirks" because we live above ground.

They threw us all out of Faerie, for unknown reasons. And even Great-aunt Gilda, the oldest of all of us, doesn't remember why. Or at least Great-aunt Gilda doesn't say. Another secret.

We, of course, just called ourselves the Family.

My Great-grandfather Fergus (according to Father) had been the first leader of the Shouting Fey. No one called Fergus a king, though in fact that's what he was. He had other titles, too: Lord of Misrule, Earl of the Downers, Father Fol-de-rol, and sometimes just plain Puck.

Great-grandfather Fergus had married Banshee, a woman of the faerie mounds, whom no one else wanted, for she was Cursed to keen loudly at the waterside whenever there was to be a death of kings and their kin. Faerie kings as well as human kings, which may be why Fergus refused the title. He reportedly said, "If I am no king, she will never have to keen me down."

Dusty once said that made Fergus a coward and he wanted nothing more to do with him, but at that point he'd never himself had anything to be truly brave about except an iron bar.

I said back, "Great-grandfather Fergus sounds less like someone afraid and more as if he was just terribly in love with his wife and didn't want her to suffer."

*Dusty answered witheringly, "*You *are a romantic."*

I went right to my favorite dictionary in the D *section of the library and looked that up. We have thirteen dictionaries, enough for each of Father's children, but I'm the only one who regularly consults them.* Romantic—*it seems—is not a bad thing to be.*

Great-grandfather Fergus was evidently a romantic, too. He'd fallen in love with Banshee's long white-gold hair and her black shroud eyes. He nearly wept tears of pearl at her lovely voice. "Like an angel," said the folks who'd obviously never heard her keening. When Banshee wasn't keening by a river in a voice that could shatter glass, she spoke softly, even sweetly. In fact, some folk called her a "Fallen Angel," which is what people say when they can't think of something nicer.

However, "keening" is a pretty way of putting what Banshee did. When Great-aunt Gilda told stories about her, she said that Banshee's voice was somewhere between the wail of a grieving woman and the moan of an owl, appropriate for someone whose chief job is to announce the deaths of kings before they happen.

It was because of Great-grandmother Banshee, of course, that we got to be known as the Shouting Fey. The use of the voice for magick seemed to be the one trait that bred true in the Family. Banshee's three daughters didn't keen, but all could Shout, a variation that was passed down to the rest of us, especially the girls of the Family, of whom I am the youngest.

·3·
PROPHECY AND INVITATION

My big adventure really began nine months before the human king's only child was born. I mean the human king on whose land our pavilion and belvederes and whimsies sit. I was thirteen and thought I knew a thing or three, though what followed after the royal birth proved to me that everything I'd believed before was wrong.

That birth had been long awaited, *really* long awaited. As in a dozen years or more. For the fey, that's an eyeblink. But for humans—especially for the royal kind—it's an eternity. We fey rarely die except by accident, Oath-breaking, or on purpose, and then mostly out of boredom. On the other hand, humans labor mightily to produce an heir or two before one or both parents expire, which happens early and often.

The queen of this kingdom was a harridan with a great dowry and even greater lands. Alas, she was thought to be barren, for years of that particular royal marriage had produced nothing but promises, taxes, and wars. The king might have set her aside for someone younger, prettier, quieter, who could bear him children, except then she would have taken her lands and jewels home with her. Because of her personality, even with her lands and jewels, neither her father nor brother wanted her back. But they would have been forced to go to war for the insult anyway.

Still, worried about being thrown out of the kingdom, the queen took matters into her own hands. She Bid Great-aunt Gilda come to her and bring both a potion and a Wish that would guarantee children. Now, as the queen knew, such potions and such Wishes could sometimes go awry, which is why she hadn't sent a Bidding for a child before. But she was desperate, fearing the king was already deep into negotiations to send her home. And so she Bid Great-aunt Gilda swear a terrible Oath guaranteeing a child.

So Great-aunt Gilda had had to swear because of the Bidding. But she knew that there could be no guarantee.

Magick simply doesn't work that way. Sometimes you get exactly the opposite of what you expected, especially if something like a Bidding or an Oath is involved. So when she got home, Great-aunt Gilda called us all to a family meeting in front of her house. She was dressed in her best purple robes, which quieted the trembling of her wings. There was an odd pallor to her face, though normally she was rosy-cheeked and the picture of health.

"My dears," she said, her voice low, which was also unusual, "I have had to swear an Oath this day to guarantee the queen will soon be with child."

We all gasped. We knew the odds.

"So I have called you together to tell you my Will."

I was all atremble. In the thirteen fey years I'd been alive, no one in the Family had ever died or even had to tell us their Will because of sickness, accident, or a coming duel. My headaches and agues were simply not thought to be life-threatening enough and besides, as the youngest, I hadn't very much to give away.

So it was clear that Great-aunt Gilda thought she might not be successful with the queen's baby. And, if she wasn't successful, the Oath would be compromised, and she'd burst into a thousand stars. I tried to hold back my tears, but they were already gathering in the corners of my eyes.

"Being of sound Fey mind," she began, "I bequeath all that I have to the Family. Gardenia can have my belvedere, because she's stuck in the smallest folly which still leaks, despite all we've done to fix it, though there's this proviso: every one of her sisters gets to choose a keepsake, and after them, the grandlings. The girls (by which she meant Mother's sisters) may have my everyday robes and dresses, except for these purple robes, which go to Galda, who is the eldest, and Banshee's Cloak of Invisibility, which—if found—shall go to Grete as the seventh, and after her, to *her* youngest, Gorse, the thirteenth."

Beside me, Solange drew in a harsh breath, for surely she, as the seventh child of a seventh child, should have been getting the Cloak and not me.

Either Great-aunt Gilda hadn't heard that sharp intake of breath or thought it beneath her to react to it at such a moment, for she simply continued telling her Will. "The boys can have Fergus's compass, knives, hats, and bows, the arrows they already have. And as for you, elf . . ." She turned to Father, who stood stony-faced in the back of our group. I looked over my shoulder at him. "There are three books in my belvedere from Banshee's time, and you may have them for your library, where they may do more good than sitting on my shelf."

Father looked stunned. I supposed he hadn't known about the books. I smiled tremulously at him, and only then did the tears slip down my cheeks.

Great-aunt Gilda squared her shoulders, bid us good

day, and went back into her belvedere, shutting the door very solidly behind her.

We were all too shocked to speak and so dispersed to our private places, each and every one of us, without saying what we were thinking.

Yet not a day later, after taking the potion that Great-aunt Gilda concocted for her, the queen went bathing in a mountain stream with her ladies-in-waiting, more for the sake of cooling than cleanliness. Mostly humans are a disgustingly filthy lot.

And a frog—or so the queen said—climbed upon her royal knee and prophesied that she would have a child.

Now, I have known many frogs. And though the peepers especially are a solipsistic tribe, believing they alone bring up spring from the edge of the world, frogs have no magickal talents at all.

None.

And they usually don't speak to humans.

"Unless they're enchanted princes, of course," Dusty whispered to me when we heard. "But even then, they can't tell the future."

He was right, of course, as he often was. But wrong, too. As he can often be.

The human ability to believe the unbelievable is legendary.

In rapid succession, they can believe the world rests on the backs of giant turtles and that the stars sing out in spheres. They believe that angels guide their days and that aliens from faraway worlds live among them—who also guide their days. They can believe 101 things that no fey would ever consider without first checking out the rumors, possibilities, and downright lies.

The queen heard the knee-creature out, leaped from the stream, and rushed off home, her crown on her head and precious little else on. We know this because Bobbin and Robbin had been spying on her. Or rather spying on her pretty handmaidens, and didn't the Aunts ream the two of them out afterward.

Once at the palace, in a high, breathy voice, the queen told the king of the prophecy, though she conveniently left out the Bidding, the potion, the Wish, and the Oath. The king wouldn't have been happy about the Oath. If he was careful about one thing, it was keeping us Shouting Fey alive.

The king, though well past believing her promises, was not above hope. In fact, he hoped for a month and then lost faith all over again.

Faith twice broken is hard mending, Father likes to say.

But much to everyone's surprise—except Father's—the queen gave birth some nine and a half months later, huffing and puffing and screaming almost as loudly as a Shouting Fey.

Gave birth to a girl.

Father said, "There is a law to be enacted years hence called Probability, and it means that occasionally a frog's prophecy will have to be accurate."

"What law?" roared Great-aunt Gilda, no longer pale and quiet as she'd been for months until the news of the queen's baby had been announced with a rather large bottle of champagne in a basket addressed to her and delivered by three footmen in full livery. The Oath, you see, had been fulfilled.

"I have it in a book somewhere. Shall I get it for you?" Father asked, which was always an effective way to stop a conversation with Great-aunt Gilda, who huffed out of our pavilion and back to her belvedere, muttering about the difference between possibilities and probabilities to anyone who would listen.

Robbin and Bobbin went off spying again and came back with the news that the king, staring down at the little bundle wrapped in a pink blanket, had announced, "Now that we know my beloved wife is not barren, she will soon have a second child. A boy this time."

When Father heard that, he shook his head. "That kind

of encouragement only leads to bad behavior." And then he added, "Poor king. He doesn't understand the power of women. Or their desires. Or how perfect and perfectly wonderful girl children can be."

The king and queen called the princess Talia, a lovely name for what was a homely, bawling, squawling infant. I'd flown into the palace, snuck into her bedroom, and peeked at her one night when even the nursemaids had fallen asleep, exhausted from her constant demands.

Red-faced from her latest screaming bout, Talia lay in her golden cradle, eyes closed and all but naked, having kicked off her covers. A silken blankie had been flung halfway out. Who knew human babies had such strength?

A silver rattle lay next to her head. I considered flying down and covering her up again, less to make her warm than to put that belly out of sight. I thought about placing the rattle in her fat little fingers. Or bonking her on the nose with it. I even thought about tickling her feet.

And then she opened her eyes, saw me, and started to scream again. It was louder than Great-aunt Gilda's worst Shout, without any magick in it at all. Just anger or frustration or royal temper, or a combination of all three. It nearly shattered my eardrums. And it did not auger well for the young woman she would become.

I shuddered and flew right back home. There I lay on my bed for a day and a half with a blistering headache that no tisane could touch. The baby princess had no magick, but she sure had lungs.

Several weeks later, the king Bid the Family to come to Talia's christening and bring her, each one of us, a valuable and magickal gift. He was quite specific. He wanted gifts of fabulous beauty and a soft voice to be numbered in our giving, which made sense, since right at the moment, anyone could see she had neither. He also wanted sweetness of character, an ability to enchant the masses, the brains of a scribe, and the ability to pluck music from a harp. And much, much more.

The usual stuff.

The Bidding looked like an ordinary royal invitation, written in gold leaf. The king's scribe had decorated the tops and bottoms with babies and crowns, and a smattering of harebells painted in odd, unnatural colors, as if the man had simply never seen one up close. Harebells, that is, not babies. There was a purple ribbon wrapping the invitation into an inviting scroll. Inviting, that is, if we'd been angling for an invite.

But this was no ordinary summons, as the messenger who delivered it made sure we understood. It was a Royal Bidding.

By custom—and the laws of magick—none of us could refuse.

Remember, I was thirteen and as contrary as any thirteen-year-old. I was no longer quite as quiet as I'd been as a child, though still accident-prone. I now used the library to find out as much as I could about the world outside of our small kingdom, and wanted nothing more than to be away from the close confines of our life here. After all, I was learning about everything I could, from coprolite and bat guano to Darwinism and entropy. I tried cookbooks in the hopes of understanding what this chocolate I'd been reading about could possibly be. I'd even borrowed the Archimedes book from Dusty, reading passages over and over again till the book was threadbare. I was only up to the *H*'s in the bookshelves, but then I was only thirteen.

As I flew home one day in a long, slow soar from the meadow, where I often went to read books aloud because that usually helped me understand the hard parts, I happened to glance down just as the king's messenger in his red-and-gold uniform arrived at our front door. I could see the bald spot on his head, round as a bull's-eye, and stifled the urge to drop one of the books on it, *All About Iron*. It was a boring book, and it seemed from above that he was sure to be a boring man. They deserved one another.

I watched as he shifted awkwardly, first on one leg and

then the other, as if he were some kind of stork. He looked uncomfortable and afraid; most humans do when trespassing in our woods. Every once in a while, he leaned forward and tentatively rapped his knuckles on the door, which no one ever does, and so no one heard him. Or if they did, they assumed he was a woodpecker. Finally, he leaned even farther forward, nose almost on the door, searching—I supposed—for an iron knocker, though we, of course, had none, iron being anathema to the fey, though the book on iron never mentioned it. So much for *All About*.

I flew down, startling him, though he stood his ground. As frightened as he was of me (they are told that we eat human children for our Christmas breakfast), he was much more afraid of what the king would do to him if he didn't deliver the invitation.

I landed badly and hurt my ankle, but it was nothing compared to other landings I have had. This time, I didn't even let out a moan.

"Mistress," he said (actually, I was not yet old enough for such address, but messengers are sticklers for good form), "the king sends you his greetings and a Bidding."

"What is it?" I asked, pointing at the scroll. "His greetings or the Bidding or something else?"

"I am . . ." And then he was taken by such a severe cough, I had to wait several minutes to hear the rest of his answer.

When the spasms stopped, he said in a bruised and shaky voice, "I am not of the privilege or class to know what is in the Royal Scroll." He said it as if it was in capital letters. I suspected he couldn't read, being only a messenger.

"I"—at that, he almost started coughing all over again, but managed to gulp it back down—"can only give it to one of the Shouting Fey. The king Bids them come and gift his new daughter with beauty, a soft voice, sweetness of character, the brains of a scribe, and a fine ear for music."

He looked at me carefully to be sure I was indeed one of the Family. I suppose the wings gave me away. And the fact that I had just dropped down from the sky.

"Do you need to come in?" I asked, taking the scroll from him.

He squeaked, "No. I am just . . . following orders." And before I could ask anything more, he had turned and was gone, running out of the woods as fast as his legs could take him.

I brought the scroll inside to Mother, who was in the kitchen with Father having a cup of steamy mulberry wine even though it was early afternoon.

She unrolled the scroll with a sigh.

Standing in front of her, I could easily read the Bidding upside down, a trick I'd learned over the years with Father in the library. He watched me and knew what I was doing.

"Gorse . . . " he warned, but it was too late. I'd already scanned the entire contents. The scribe's writing was *very* big, with nothing much else to commend it, especially its lack of punctuation.

As the king of all shires here
around and further
I Bid the entire Court of the Shouting Fey
to come to the christening of
Talia
Princess Royal Duchess of Coventry
Lady of Wellington Wells
and Airdel of the Seven Hills
The christening starts Monday next at 8 am
Appropriate gifts are mandatory
Do not be late

I was appalled. "He clearly never met a comma or period he liked."

Mother said, "What?"

Father smiled wanly.

And then I realized what the message actually said. I made a face. "Why did he Bid *us*? He's got all those cousins and hangers-on and in-laws and outlaws who can come with gifts," I said. "And we're so poor, we're forced to live on moonbeams and drink dew and . . ."

It wasn't really true of course, but lovely in its own way. I'd borrowed the moonbeams and dew stuff from Great-aunt Gilda, who in full rant could go on like that for hours.

Mother shook her head. She was one Shout away from blasting me back into my room, though I doubted she would waste her daily Shout on such small stuff. Still, she stiffened and her head snapped up. "He will want us to confer such attributes as—"

"I already *know* that," I broke in sassily.

She looked at Father and said four words to him, the same four she'd used when any of her children reached the Age of Argumentation, as she called it.

"You . . . speak . . . to . . . her." She struck her middle finger on the table for each syllable with such force, the cups of wine nearly fell off the tabletop. Her mouth looked pinched, as if she'd been sucking on lemons, and her normally gooseberry-green eyes were suddenly black as shrouds. "Innocence is all very well and good, and I know she's the baby and your favorite and you've insisted on keeping her in the dark about family stuff while educating her far beyond what can be found in our borders, but honestly, my love, you've left this one for too long."

· 4 ·

TIED

Innocence. Mother had thrown the word between them as if it were so filthy, it hurt her mouth to say it. But if she meant by "innocence" that I'd been left unschooled in matters that I should have known about, I agreed. Secrets are one thing, but intentional stupidity another.

Father drew me out of the kitchen, down the hall, and into the library. His touch was soft, but there was no denying the steel beneath. I'd never actually noticed that steel before. Strangely enough, it was comforting.

With its floor-to-ceiling shelves and cozy divans and chairs, the library was usually a sanctuary. But it was cold that day, and the room was full of shadows. *They* should have served as a warning. Or if I'd more magick at that pivotal age, I might have guessed the truth.

We sat between the *N*'s for *Neverland* and the *O*'s for *Ontology* and *Oz*. Not having read past the *H*'s yet, I had no idea what those things were, though *Ontology* had a lovely lilt to it. I wasn't so sure about *Neverland*, which sounded awfully negative.

My back was as rigid as Mother's had been. "Why must we spend our remaining bits of magick on some stupid human baby?" I said in that challenging way thirteen-year-olds have. "Just because a stupid king *Bids* it!" I waved a hand in the general direction of the castle, or at least in what I thought was the general direction of the castle, though I was a full ninety degrees off. The library, being round and in the very center of the pavilion, often had that effect on my understanding of the compass points.

"I mean," I continued, "we have nothing, and the king has a million acres of land. He has six rivers, five mountains, and the tithing of all the farms from the Western Sea to the East." This last I'd heard Great-aunt Gilda say. My hand was still waving about like a compass needle gone mad.

"A *quarter* million," Father said.

"A million, a quarter million, what's the difference? It's still a lot!" I crossed my arms and grumped. I'd gotten very good at grumping lately.

"Think, Gorse, think," Father said. It was something he was always saying to me, but never to my brothers and sisters, as if I were the only one deficient in thinking. "In a spell, any kind of numerical discrepancy makes a *huge* difference." Father's face was solemn. "Which you know." Then he added even more softly, "And in life as well, my darling girl."

My mouth curled downward, like a parenthesis. Calling me his *darling girl* did nothing to pull me from my grump, even if I was—in Mother's astonishing word—his *favorite*. But I was determined to let him know. "Well, it's *not* a spell. And it's *not* fair."

Father smiled at me. "Of course it's not fair. And even *less* fair than you know. That's what Mother wants me to tell you."

"No she doesn't."

"Just listen for once, Gorse, and think," Father said. "I know that's hard to do at thirteen."

And then I remembered the other word. "What did she mean by innocence?"

He sighed. "Your mother learned what I am about to tell you when she was so young, it ruined her childhood. I determined it would not happen to any of you, and with you being the last, and so often ill, I wanted to let you still have a time of *not* knowing—"

"You of all people to say that, Father."

His long face looked even longer, and he ran a hand through his hair, disclosing his elf ears, a sign that he was really distressed. "Hear me out, child. I had thought, you see, to have discovered how to change things long before you got this old. But . . ."

I tried to look as if I were *not* listening. I played with my hair, twining strands around my fingers. Once Father had tried to explain to me why I was the only one with black hair, why Alliford the only one with red hair. The explanation had letters in it—RNB or DNO or something—but it was another of those not-fair things, and I'd refused to listen. He'd even tried to tell me it had to do with peas in a pod, and that had made no sense at all.

I looked up at the cupola, where last year's autumn leaves still lay dark and sodden against the glass.

"This is important, dear child," he said.

I made another face. "So important you deliberately kept it from me?"

He put his hands on mine. "*Really* important that you listen now."

So I listened. Father doesn't use the qualifier "really" often. And of course I *really* wanted to know what he had to say. So, I leaned in toward him, and he knew he'd gotten my full attention.

His voice got quiet and solemn. "Now, you know all *about* Biddings. But you don't know the *why* of them. So I am going to tell you that, but a lot more, too."

"Is this true, or a story?" I wasn't going to let the grump go very easily, even though I knew Father couldn't lie.

"Perhaps a bit of both," Father said, "since I am telling you what the Aunts and your mother have told me." He smiled sadly. "The story is the sweetener."

I nodded. And listened.

"Now," Father began, "the king owns many acres of land. He can ride out as he wills. He can conquer more acres if he wishes. He can have a summer house on a far island and go on long trips to the Continent. He taxes people as much as he can, and when he can't, he sometimes imprisons them and takes their homes or starts wars. He can even marry again if his wife displeases him."

I waved a hand dismissively. "She displeases *me*," I said. "She's a whiner and—"

"Hush," Father said.

I hushed.

He pulled me into his comforting arms, all but whispering in my ear. "But have you never wondered why we of the Family never go on long trips, beyond the borders of this kingdom? Why we have never visited ancient monuments in the Far East or the new building in the West? Why we have not moved on from this glade?"

“We love it here, Father,” I said. “It’s home.” Though just earlier I’d been longing for far-off climes.

“Yes, we love it. And yes, it *is* our home. But that is not the reason.”

I stayed silent until Father, taking a deep breath, said, “We are tied to this land and cannot remove from it.”

I eased out of his sheltering arms and turned to stare at him, thinking that perhaps this was the story part or that he was making a joke. Not a particularly funny joke, though. But I knew that besides always telling the truth, elves are incapable of telling jokes. Though they *can* laugh. He was not laughing now. His face held the seriousness with which he spoke of True Things.

I bit my bottom lip. How could this tied-to-the-land thing be true? Hadn’t Father lived in Eire before he married Mother, somewhere over the Easter Sea?

Almost as if he had read my mind—though mind reading is not an elvish trait either—he said, “Once I married your Mother and we had our family, I became tied to the land as well. Family is what we have when everything else is gone.”

“Tied?”

“Tied with bonds of magick as old and secure as Common Law.”

I already knew about Common Law. Father had explained it recently when we were talking about highwaymen because I'd found them in a book under *H*. Common Law was what had been accepted as law before things got written down, before people—fey or human—had begun to write. It's *that* old.

"But, Father—"

His dark eyes got darker, and he held up a hand. "Hush. We owe our fortunes—"

"What fortunes?"

A finger to his lips to shush me. "We owe our fortunes, such as they are, our long existence, such as it is, and the lives of our children to the rulers of this land. The original king took in Fergus and Banshee when no one else would, after they'd been thrown out by the other fey and had wandered around the countryside, camping by wells, couching in cowsheds, squatting in abandoned houses. And there they were, without protection, the two of them and their young family—they had two little daughters by then."

"Gemma and Gerna?"

He nodded. "And they all could have been killed by humans easily, for their Shouting ability was not yet honed and they'd lost most of their magick coming above the Hill. Besides, Gerna was still an infant, and you know, I think, that a nursing fey woman is essentially without magick.

But our king's great-, great-, seven-times-great grandfather made a bargain with Fergus and Banshee. He said,

'You stay here under our protection and do a Bidding when we need it, which we will consider as binding as an Oath, and you will never be harmed by me or mine.'"

"Ah," I said, not yet *quite* understanding.

Father ran his tongue over his upper lip, for his mouth had gone dry with the telling. "Over the centuries, custom has made that exchange into unbreakable law, and the Biddings—though in recent times capricious and unnecessary—have become our duty. We are bounden to do a Royal Bidding whether we agree with it or not."

I leaned forward, now trembling with anger. "I've known about the Biddings for as long as I can remember, Father. But, *tied* . . ."

I thought of all the places I'd read about: the Hanging Gardens of Babylon, the Hellespont, China's Great Wall like the spine of a dragon, the Eiffel Tower, The Golden Gate Bridge: things from the past, the present, the future. Was I never to see any of them? Not the geysers of the world, the Grand Canyon, the blue ice of the frozen Alaska, the Andes Mountains, the Alps? And I hadn't even gotten beyond the *H*'s yet.

He shook his head. "I know, I know, darling child. During all the time I have been here, and before that as well, the Shouting Fey have been tied to this land. The royals could withdraw their protection and let us go. We are certainly strong enough now to withstand living outside of this domain without fear. But as long as the present royal family remains in power, can you see any of them voluntarily giving us up? They count on our magicks and spend them unwisely. But we made a promise. And a fey who goes back on an Oath . . ."

I whispered, "Bursts into a thousand stars." I lifted my arms and made a motion with my fingers like stars falling, or rain. Then I thought a minute. "Is that *true*? I mean, we all say it as though it's true, but has it ever *actually* happened? Not just in a story?"

He held out his hand and drew me to him again, which made me think he knew that what he had to say next was going to shock me or move me or both. So I let him pull me in.

"There were not seven but *eight* children in your Mother's immediate family: the seven girls—"

"Mother and the Aunts," I said, and he nodded. "Who all looked like their beautiful Mother, Gerne." It was an old family story, but a good one.

"And a lovely, smart boy named Goldenrod."

"A boy? Nobody ever said there was a boy." I was astonished.

"He was the oldest, and when he turned seventeen, he said to the Family at dinner, '*We* never took that Oath to the king, you know. It doesn't apply to us, only Grandmother and Grandfather.' He meant Fergus and Banshee, of course."

"Of course," I whispered, hoping Father would stop right there. But he didn't.

"Goldenrod set off down the path with Galda and your Mother, who was just five, trailing after him, begging him to turn back. He got as far as the road to Marbleton, which was then a separate kingdom. And no sooner had he set foot beyond the borders of the kingdom, than he . . ." Father stopped, took a deep breath.

"He *didn't* burst . . ."

Father nodded. "They watched until the last star had faded from sight, then trudged home, too stunned to weep until they were safe in their mother's arms. She died soon after. They all believed that the shock killed her. And not six human months later, in his deep grief, their father—who was a human—died, too."

I, too, was shocked, but I didn't weep. I'd never known Grandmother and Grandfather, and as for Uncle Goldenrod, not till this very moment had I even heard of him. Though Aunt Galda had taught us all a jump rope rhyme that went:

Goldenrod on the road,
Golden stars all explode,

Skip to the left, skip to the right,
Take one step and out of sight.

Out of sight, indeed. It had never occurred to me that the rhyme celebrated a tragedy in the Family. I'd always thought it was a nursery rhyme about a flower spreading its seed. I wasn't going to weep. I couldn't weep. I was too angry for that.

"Was there *ever* a time that the kings of the kingdom were good to us?"

"Oh, sweet child, Carmody the First saved Fergus and Banshee, which means he saved the Family. He told them that they must never go outside his borders because he could only protect them within his kingdom, and they swore they would not. And he further asked them to swear to come when he Bid them, so he could keep an eye on them and be sure they were all right."

"They *swore*?" I gasped.

"Yes, Gorse, they swore an Oath for their entire family. And though Carmody was a good king for all of his life and never actually Bid them do anything, that Oath has stood all these years."

So we'd done this to ourselves, to all our descendants for . . . well, forever, I supposed, and said so, loudly and with passion.

"King Carmody never knew that a fey Oath means

something more than a human Oath," Father said, "which means next to nothing."

I thought of my Uncle Goldenrod, and those thousand stars. I thought of Aunt Galda and Mother as a young child watching what happened. "And the other kings?" My voice had gone very soft.

"His son Crom was a very wise ruler who built a great library. But he knew about the Oath and what it meant. He'd read about it in one of his books. When he was an old, old man—he lived to be nearly a hundred, as had his father—I came through the kingdom on a visit to some far-flung relatives who lived across the border, though really I wanted to visit that library. It was quite famous by that time. Of course, that's when I met your mother, and I never got to see my birth family again."

"A library . . ." I mused.

"Yes, I became the king's librarian for the rest of his rule. We spent many happy hours discussing books, the king and I. He left me some of my favorites in his will. The rest, I'm afraid, were burned by his successor for taking up too much space, a space that he turned into a ballroom for dances and games." He shuddered. "Carmody the Second he was called and, while not a bad man, quite a stupid one. Took after his mother. He knew about the Bidding because his father had told him, and he knew about the bursting into a thousand stars as well. So began the history of the abuse of Bidding that the royal family has used on us till this very day."

He stood and began pacing while continuing his story of the Family. "Now, burning the books was ultimately disastrous for the kingdom, but at least Carmody the Second let me take the books set down for me in his father's will. I sneaked a few extra out as well. This was before I discovered the library hole. It was already in the belvedere wall. And the belvedere had been built by Old Crom, so I have often wondered . . ."

"But after that?" I held out no hope for a positive answer about the Biddings and got none.

"Alas, child, the king and his heirs since have developed into a dynasty of idiots, louts, greedyguts, and fools. In my estimation, it all comes down to burning the books. An awful fate, but there it is. No one has ever said that Fate is kind."

"Why didn't Mother want to tell me this herself?"

He took up both my hands and held them. I could feel him trembling. A lock of his thinning hair fell over one eye, giving him a piratical look. "Because, Gorse, the telling of it makes her physically ill. Not for what it means for herself, not anymore, but for what it means for me and for you children. She'd thought that, long before we had any of you, the duty to the king would have been resolved. Otherwise, she mightn't have married me and certainly wouldn't have had you children. And after that, she trusted me to find a solution, and I have failed her."

"So far, Father. But you have me to help now."

He wasn't listening. "She should have remained one of the unmarried and childless Shouters," he whispered. "It would have hurt her less."

"Like Great-aunt Gilda," I whispered back, reaching out and catching his hand. But I didn't want to believe him. Believing him would mean that I'd been mistaking Mother all these years. Ever since that conversation I'd overheard, I'd thought she hadn't married Father for love, when now I clearly understood that she had.

And yet, I *did* believe him. And believing, I forgave her entirely.

Father kissed me on the brow and walked out of the library to let me think. I sat there until the light faded and evening settled in around the pavilion, the home that now felt an awful lot like a prison.

For hours, the phrase *we are tied to the land* ran full circle around my brain, and it was not a comforting thought. The Biddings were an annoyance, a tithing, and we were sworn to them. But to be tied to one place by law and not by choice was a hateful thing. So was the knowledge that there was nothing I could do about those ties.

During the following hours, I would think, *There has to be something.* And find a bit of hope. Then as suddenly my traitor brain would counter, *It's always been this way. Even Father says so, and he has not found anything to break that tie.* And then all hope was dashed. Round and round I went.

The moon rose, and a shaft pierced the gloom, like a prophecy. Suddenly I remembered the *actual* prophecy, which I hadn't given any brain space to in years. That's when I understood for the first time why Mother and the Aunts had so wanted me to be the One:

The One comes into the daylight veiled,
So long awaited, hoped for, hailed
Where others tried and always failed.
And from a deep and darkened space,
A Savior of an ancient race,
The One will, wingless, come apace.
With brand-new wings, the One can fly,
Makes truth come out of ancient lie,
So severs bonds and every tie.

"Severs bonds and every tie." I said it aloud. "They meant that literally. And I failed them."

Had *I* not tried hard enough?

I'd already forgiven Mother, but that was much easier than forgiving myself, something I didn't even try, at least not then. Not till much, much later.

But I did weep, long into the night, long past the setting of the moon. I wept for the Family and for me. And for Father, who hadn't been born this way but had chosen it out of love.

I think I wept for Father most of all.

Once I'd finished weeping, I sneaked around the pavilion, spying on everyone. My brothers and sisters were all asleep, which seemed unjust to me. Surely they'd already known about being tied to the land, and no one had ever thought to warn me. One little warning, maybe, like, "Gorse, there's something you should know." I mean, they passed on every other little bit of gossip and innuendo that came their way. The boys were the worst, actually.

Or perhaps, I thought, *this is just a rite of passage. If no one else had thought to warn me, why hadn't Dusty? He was not just my big brother, he was my best friend.*

I could *almost* hear his voice, saying, *About to turn thirteen, Goosey? You have a tremendous surprise in store!* Almost, but not quite, since he'd never said a blessed word.

Gritting my teeth, I kept sneaking about the pavilion,

tiptoeing from room to room, getting angrier by the moment. Suddenly I heard a strange sound, something between a wind wuthering and a crow's call. I followed it, as if it were a thread that needed winding up, and found myself standing before Mother and Father's bedroom.

Only then did I realize the sound was Mother crying.

I don't think I'd ever actually heard her crying before, at least not like this—harsh and unending.

I stood for a long time listening, until there was a whisper from Father.

"Darling girl," he said.

I'd never heard him call *her* that. That was what he called *me*! This was a strange time, with new revelations at every turning.

"Darling girl, keep your voice low. Please don't Shout."

"I . . . am . . . not . . . Shouting," she said. She wept between each word. "You would *know* if I were Shouting. The children would know. The Aunts would know. *Everyone* would know." She gulped back another sob. "Mab's breath, even that disgusting king would know IF I WERE SHOUTING!"

She was right. But he was right, too.

"For the children's sake," he said.

"It's *for* their sake that I'm crying."

"Still . . ." He didn't finish the sentence, but she knew—even *I* knew—what he meant.

She swallowed the cries. "But it's not *fair*."

"You sound just like Gorse."

That shut her up entirely.

After some long, tense moments, the silence was so deafening, I left and went outside. After all I had to think about, sleep was not an option.

I fluttered down the hill to the little meadow that was my refuge. Lying in the dewy grass, I gazed up at the night sky. The moon was all but gone, though I could still see the three stars of Mab's Crown showing directly above me and, off to the right, the cluster Father calls Puck's Handkerchief. As I watched, there were some quick flashes of light as asteroids sped across the dark bowl of the heavens. I'd learned about them years ago, in the Astronomy section of the library. Comforted by the familiar far-away, exhausted from all the new feelings and frustrations I'd discovered, I fell asleep in the grass and did not wake till long past dawn.

Of course, when I awoke, my nose was running, my eyes streamed as fast as any little brook, and my forehead blazed with yet another ague.

I trudged home and put myself to bed. Every bone in my body felt miserable, and that seemed about right. After all, I knew sickness. Understood it. It was a familiar upset. Not like that *other* thing.

I refused to think any more about being tied to the land.

·5·

GIFTS

In the morning, the Family was to gather in the dining hall to discuss the possibilities of what each of us could bring to the christening. And the morning after that, we were to go up to the castle.

I wasn't there, of course. It turned out I was horribly sick with fever, my body racked with alternate hot and cold shivers rushing like a spring spate across my skin. Who would have believed that a single starry night in a wet field should become so important to the fate of us all?

As I lay sipping the hot tisane that Father had made for me—trying not to shake it all over the bedclothes and my nightdress with my trembling hand—I knew Mother and Father, my brothers and sisters, cousins and Aunts were all in the Great Hall of Great-aunt Gilda's belvedere, receiving the few implements of Old Magick we had to use at the princess's christening.

I was simply too sick to care. If I could have lifted my head from the pillow, I might have cried out for help. But that was not going to happen till the fever broke. I lay felled by ague and something else.

I think it was relief.

Vivid fever dreams haunted me. I saw carts running along iron tracks. I heard the rustle of paper dresses. I watched pictures moving on the front of wooden boxes. I thrilled at humans leaping off cliffs, shaking huge and oddly shaped multicolored wings before catching an updraft and flying over the flat land. All of it beyond any magick humans could possibly ever have, or so I thought. But fever dreams are not meant to be read plainly.

I slept through most of the day and night and solidly into the next morning. Things rustled around me, but my eyelids were too gummed up to try and see what they were. Nor did I have the energy to rub my lids free of the stickiness. I just lay there, listening.

In between dreams, I tried to guess what was happening by the sounds. Was Solange borrowing a hairbrush? Willow sneaking about the hallway? Were the twins playing a trick on Dusty? Was Father coming to check on me, or Great-aunt Gilda here for a scold?

The strangest dream of all was one in which Mother

came into my room to sit beside me, crooning a lullaby. *A lullaby!* How odd. She hadn't sung to me since I was small.

In my dream, she laid a cool cloth on my forehead and left a fresh tisane in our best cup by my bed. Then she kissed me on both cheeks, saying in a soft voice, "Sleep well, little one." Though I wasn't very little anymore and, as she knew only too well, I wasn't the One.

Yes, a very strange dream indeed.

And then she was gone.

When I woke, the best cup was actually sitting there, on the table by my bed, filled with a minty-smelling tisane, cold but still effective.

Had Mother actually been beside me, and not just in my dream?

Or had one of the Aunts come by and left it, and I mistook her voice for Mother's?

I didn't know, and at that moment it hardly mattered. I drank the contents down in quick gulps before falling asleep again without tasting either the peppermint or the spell.

What I didn't know was that, while I slept almost around the clock, Father had apportioned out the implements, leaving nothing in the spell trunk but an old linden spindle knotted about with the thread of a long life that was hidden by a tatty cloth.

Possibly he left it because the instruction sheet was in tatters, having been severely mouse-nibbled and shredded for nests. Or perhaps he'd never noticed it. Or perhaps, having apportioned out the best gifts for a baby princess—beauty, riches, sweetness, wit—Father hadn't given a single thought about an end-of-life spell spun out on a wooden distaff.

Or perhaps he left it there for me, in the hope that I'd be up in time.

All I knew was that, while I slept away my fever, the Family had gone off to the christening without me.

Since I'd been included in the Bidding, there was real danger not just to me but to the Family. We could individually or all together burst into a thousand stars if the king or queen noticed. I wondered briefly that no one had wakened me or carried me off to the palace wrapped in a blanket, so I would at least be there to be counted, whether I could make a gift or not.

But Aunt Galda, being an occasional far-seer, must have known I'd be up in time. I refused to think that this might be one of the moments her far-seeing fluttered and failed. She'd evidently been more reliable when young, according to Solange, who got all her information from the Aunts.

However, as I was still alive, I supposed that there was nothing more that could be done, except hope that neither the king nor queen were able to count.

•

When I finally woke again, I felt cool but extremely parched and whimpered for some more peppermint tea.

No one but the three doves in the rafters answered me. *Co-co-roo,* they said together softly, in their apologetic voices. *Co-co-roo.*

Now, my brother Arian is the one who really understands doves. I think it's because he's slow and quiet and so doesn't frighten wild things the way the rest of us do. I'm not too bad on Crow and Jay, and love to converse in Hawk, but for one reason or another, I've never really learned Dove. They have hardly anything interesting to say, and they say it slowly. Still, I understood enough. They were telling me that the Family had gone.

"Gone?" I sat up groggily. "Gone!" I rubbed my sticky eyes, suddenly awake enough to remember where.

And why.

So I rose from my sickbed and slipped on a silvery, glittery party dress. It had once been Solange's and didn't fit me particularly well, as I was not so full-figured as she. But I didn't care. The dress shimmered, and that was all that would matter to the king's court, though the Family would know at once that the shimmer came mostly from the spiderweb patches. Solange is so hard on her clothes. But none of that mattered. All that mattered was that I get to the castle before the king or queen started to count.

When I looked in the glass, my hair seemed startled into place. I combed it down with my fingers, not having time to search for my brush. Then I ran into Solange's room to borrow her silver hair bow. She must have worn it to the christening herself, so I raced back to my own room and took one of my red ribands and tied it quickly around my hair, managing an almost-presentable mare's tail, and then started out of the house.

The doves *co-co-roo*ed again, nannylike in their warnings, their message very clear. It was one word, over and over and over again.

"Gift!" I'd almost forgotten the most important thing. I began to shiver, not from fever but from fear.

What if I'd arrived *without* a gift? The king would probably order Father exorcised by his priests, since elves don't burst from broken Oaths. Only the fey do. But bursting into stars is not nearly as painful as exorcism, or so I've heard. In exorcism, the elf's essence is drawn out and then captured in a bottle. And Father would have to watch as the rest of us burst into stars.

I tried to imagine my dear, gentle Father corked up in a bottle for as long as the king or his kin liked. One of Father's brothers had been exorcised by a Kilkenny abbot long before Father ever married Mother. He was still locked up in a dusty carafe labeled *Bordeaux, '79.* That bottle sits on the back shelf of a monastery wine cellar and, as Father explains, whenever he tells us the story, "'79 was a terrible year for wines." Since only a human can uncork Uncle Finn, and no one will want that particular debased wine, we all thought he'd remain corked up for . . . well, forever.

I tried to imagine Father that way, peering out of a green glass bottle, looking peaked and lonely and very, very sad.

Sometimes an imagination *is* a Curse.

I ran down into the storeroom in Great-aunt Gilda's belvedere, where the trunk with the Old Magick implements stood. Sturdy and oaken, it had a fine-grained pinewood key, but the key was only for show. The trunk was bolted with a family spell, one we'd all been forced to memorize in childhood.

Come, thou, cap and lid,
Lift above what has been hid.
All out!

Of course, the last two words were done in the Shouting voice, though not a full Shout, which could have brought down the roof on my head or at least covered me with a fine dust and dove droppings. Not a good look for a christening. Still, as with all magick echoes in the storeroom, the spell made my head hurt even more, though when the final note of the Minor Shout died away, the trunk snapped open with a loud click.

I peered in and at first thought it was actually empty, But when I felt around, my hand touched something long and wooden. I picked it up and realized it was the spindle on which the Thread of Long Life was wound and that there was a rather large piece of cloth hanging from the bottom end. Briefly, I wondered why I hadn't noticed either spindle or cloth before. Just then, as if it were a trick of the light, the cloth began to disappear and so did the bottom part of the spindle.

Suddenly, I realized what I was holding. "Banshee's Cloak of Invisibility!" I whispered in awe, though it was only a piece of it. Just as I had that thought, the Cloak began to fail around the edges, turning a brown color as if it had been scorched in a fire, and suddenly I could see both the cloth and the tip of the spindle again.

"Blessed Loireg," I said with a sigh, praising my long-dead Great-great-aunt, patroness of Hebridean spinners and spinsters.

Clutching both spindle and Cloak to my breast—you never know when an Invisibility Cloak will be helpful, even if it's only an unreliable rag—I ran out of the pavilion and along the winding paths toward the castle. Since it was morning and I was still weak with fever and now had a headache as well, I didn't dare fly. Especially with all the family healers off at the christening.

As I ran, I said a small Foot Spell to speed my feet. And a tiny Calves Spell to keep my legs strong. And a minuscule Heart Spell to keep me happy. And a teensy Lung Spell that I should not run out of breath. I was magicked from one end to the other, which only served to intensify my headache. But it *had* to be done. I needed speed. And even though I knew it was Forbidden, I headed off onto the Wooing Path because, after all, it *was* the straightest line to the castle.

I'd wrapped the Cloak about my head and shoulders for warmth, and so—on and off—I was invisible as I went along. A cacophony of cows in a field near the Path noticed me, a scramble of squirrels did not. A bear pawing honey from a tree startled when I suddenly popped into view, and he dropped the bit of honeycomb he was holding onto his foot, which annoyed him very much. He growled as if to chastise me, but I didn't speak Bear, and I didn't stop running, since I feared I was going to be late. He stopped chasing me when I went invisible again.

The sun already sat high in the sky, the morning hurtling towards noon. The christening would have begun closer to cock's crow. I thought to make up some of the time with a small spell and was just figuring out which one, when I tripped over the old iron bar that Dusty had magickally shoved against a tree so very long ago. As my leg touched the bar, it burned me.

Suddenly I remembered what I'd forgot: a spell for concentration. Without concentration, a disastrous fall had been all but inevitable. Especially for one as accident-prone as I.

As I tumbled down, I lost my hair ribbon, tore a piece off Solange's silvery dress, kept hold of the spindle and Cloak, and never hit the ground. Instead, I fell into a hole at the bottom of the tree.

"Curses!" I cried, without actually Cursing anything, since Father had all but forbidden us that, though he'd never said why. All the while, I was thinking that it was surely just a small hollow in the tree. I worried more about breaking the spindle or losing the Cloak, as well as being late to the christening and ruining Solange's silver dress, when I should have been worrying about something infinitely worse.

As I fell into it, the hole yawned open, and suddenly I knew I'd been caught by a magick trap. But now it was far too late to fight my way out. I thought with a heavy sigh: *no wonder the Wooing Path had been forbidden.*

And no wonder none of the Uncles ever came back to us. It wasn't lack of love that kept them away, or the fact that human men don't live as long as the fey. It was suddenly clear that most—if not all of them—had been caught in this trap. Or maybe another just like it.

I bet the entire Wooing Path is catacombed with such things, I thought. *As soon as I get free, I'll have to tell the Aunts.* And so I dropped end over end over end over end through the blackness.

I tried to unfurl my wings, but they—of course—were caught up in the Cloak around my shoulders, and I was holding tight to the spindle and only had the use of one hand, so when I finally hit bottom, out I went once again, not with fever this time but with a bang.

Part II

UNDER THE HILL

Under the hill, the faerie kin
Sing their chants, weave their spells.
Their hearts are full, their souls are thin,
They live in caves and deep, dark wells.
They eat the honey, 'void bee stings,
They drink from cups of morning dew
They dance all night in faerie rings
And sleep the day when night is through.
Do not come near, or hear our calls,
Or you'll be gaoled within our walls.

—Traditional Song

·6·
CAVE WORT

The thing about wings is that if you have them, falling never worries you. Of course landing badly does.

And I landed very badly, hard on my right side with my right wing folded awkwardly under me.

When I woke—seconds, minutes, hours later, how was I to tell?—it was to total darkness. No stars, no moons, no fireflies, not even cave luminescence. Just pure, unrelieved blackness, a burned leg that hurt, a numb right wing, and a headache that wouldn't stop.

I wondered briefly if I'd hit my head when I landed. However, it didn't hurt to the touch, just an ache as if a band of cold iron encircled it.

The blackness was what the poets mistakenly call "ebon." A night sky is ebon. The feathers of a raven are ebon. Certain tribes on the continent of Africa are ebon. I have seen pictures of them in the *A* section of one of Father's encyclopedias. All have a sheen, a shine, a bluish tint, an elegance, a grace.

Someone not particular about words might even call my hair ebon. Except my hair is just straight, inelegant, and black.

My surroundings were simply black as well.

That was how I knew two things for certain: I was now underground, possibly in a cave, and I was surrounded by magick. Only a Great Magick can make things that black. And only a Great Magick can give me that particular kind of headache.

But Father had said we were tied to the land, and of course I'd thought he meant I could never leave the world that ran between our pavilion and the castle, all those dear, familiar running, flying, soaring places.

Yet here I was, certainly no longer in Shouting Fey territory. And just as certainly, I hadn't burst into a thousand stars. So maybe that "tied to the land" thing had a little slack to it. Or else, the land *under* the king's land still legally belonged to the king. I knew I'd have to think about that some more.

But not, I assured myself, *until my head stopped hurting.*

The leg would take a few hours to start to heal, but the wing was what was really troubling.

Sitting up slowly, I reached back to feel my wing to find out if anything had been broken, for it had begun to throb with pain, though not as badly as my head, which was why I hadn't noticed it at once. With wings—like little toes—you don't actually know until you check. So I was pleased that my fingers found everything intact, no knobs or bobs sticking out awkwardly.

The Cloak may have kept the wing safe from breakage, for the primaries were still flexible and strong; the secondaries, too. I'd lost a few feathers, but they were probably loose anyway. We always lose feathers in the autumn, like trees their leaves, and new ones grow in the spring, so I wasn't really worried about *them*. But if any of the hollow wing bones had been broken, they could take many seasons to heal properly, even with one of Mother's spells or a trip to see the Faerie Doctor who lives in the bole of the ancient sycamore and knows more about wing bones that any Shouting Fey. Still, the pain was a worry, and until that stopped, flying back up the trap was not going to be an option. I would have to find another way out.

I guess I was lucky with that tumble. Except for the head and wing pain, and the burn where I'd tripped over the iron, I was remarkably fine, and I thanked the Magick Lords under my breath. I thanked Aunt Gardenia, too, who protects and looks after lost children, dogs, and the unfortunate traveler, of which I was two. Protects them when she remembers, that is. Which isn't all that often.

I got to my knees carefully, making sure I still had the Cloak around my head and shoulders, for it was perishing cold down in the underground, and only then did I realize that I had nothing in my hands.

"Mab's bones!" I whispered. I must have dropped the spindle somewhere in the blackness. At least, I hoped I'd dropped it in the blackness and hadn't left it up above where anyone human might carry it off. I was in enough trouble already without adding that to the count.

I felt around the floor carefully. After a few tense moments, I found the spindle, and luck was still with me because it was unbroken. But my hand had touched nothing else but stone. Cold, uncaring stone.

Better than coming upon a cave beast, I thought. *Better than something hugely muscled and ravenously hungry and . . .* I was beginning to frighten myself. *Think of your luck,* I scolded. *After all, nothing's broken, nobody's burst into a thousand stars.*

Yet.

That was the only thing that kept me from sinking down and sobbing uncontrollably. It never occurred to me at that moment that everyone else might have already turned into stardust and I was saved by being miles underground and away from the awful power of the Oath.

I made a sudden wry face that I was glad no one was around to see. What kind of luck sets a person down at the bottom of a cave full of magick, in the dark, with a horrible headache? My kind of luck—all bad!

Bad, bad Gorse!

I knew I had to stop that line of thinking before I frightened myself out of any magick I might employ to get me home, since flying was out. But I sent up another small prayer to the Magick Lords who were surely watching over me because, after all, I still could walk, I still had the spindle, I still had the Cloak to keep me warm. And thinking about how fortunate I was, I stood, turned, and walked into something that was big, hairy, and smelled rather like the tail end of a sick cow.

The Something put its hairy arms around me, picked me up, and growled, "Gargle, McGargle," or something like that. Then it squeezed me till I had a hard time breathing and took off at a big, walloping gallop that shook every bone in my body and made me almost drop the spindle, my Cloak, and the rest of the loose feathers from my wings.

"Stop!" I cried with what little breath was left me, but the creature didn't stop. It ran on and on through the dark as if it could see, as if it knew where it was going. As if it didn't mind crashing into stone walls, which might not hurt the creature but certainly wouldn't do me and my poor wing any good.

"Stop!" I yelled at the Something, though I hadn't enough voice to do it as an actual Shout, which might have worked to drop the creature or at least slow it down. Or it might not. I'd no idea if I could Shout loud enough to affect such a creature or if indeed my magick would work if I were not above on Shouting Fey soil. And then I would have wasted this day's Shout.

That thought, along with the bouncing, the headache, the throbbing wing, the aching leg, and the growing fear, was enough to make me feel sick again. And sick, I knew, would not serve me well.

Think, Gorse, I told myself, *think*. But in that position, it was very hard to think. So I gave myself over to fear, panic, horror, terror, and curiosity, in that order. Luckily, curiosity outlasted them all.

Since I couldn't stop the creature, I tried to see where I was. After a while, the dark seemed less black. I could distinguish gray areas between the pitchblende, a sort of mushroomy color. Of course I couldn't figure out if that gray signified stone walls or entrances between the walls, whether it was the presence of a thing or the absence. But at least I *could* see a difference.

I squirmed a bit, and then a bit more, though careful to hold on to both the spindle and the Cloak. *As soon as I win free,* I promised myself, *I'm going to get out of here.* Wherever *here* was.

The hairy, smelly Something never dropped me, but it moved me into a more comfortable position where—as if a shadow were passing by—I could just about make out its shape whenever we raced by the gray walls. I remembered a book on Art in the *A* section of the library that explained "negative space." That's what it looked like each time I caught a glimpse of the creature.

I decided the monster was a *him,* because of the smell, if nothing else. A little like my brothers after a game of All-Out Tag. In my mind, I called the creature Wort, a strong, ugly name. He was about twenty hands taller than Father, and Father is tall by elven standards. Wort had a large, roundish head, with startling, curly hair that stood out in all directions. Occasionally his yellow eyes gleamed, round and big as skipping stones. Occasionally they slanted down into cat's eyes. When Wort opened his mouth to *McGargle* again—not frequently, but several more times as we raced along—I thought I could distinguish gray teeth.

But that was all: just big hair, gleaming eyes, gray teeth,

and a body that was almost as tall as the first floor of the pavilion. Or at least that's what he looked like in negative space. Not a comforting companion, but once named and shadow-seen, not quite as frightening as before.

We galloped on and on, through the twisting, winding corridors of stone.

I didn't know where we were going or how long it would be till we got there. But we certainly were eating up the underground miles. For the first time, I began to worry about actually finding my way back. Back to the hole I'd fallen into. Back into the bright air. Back along the Wooing Path to the castle where the bawling, grizzling princess waited and my parents counted on me to be the thirteenth fey.

Back home.

Because finding the wrong exit might be as dangerous as never getting out at all.

As we went along, I pretended I was riding Wort, rather than think about how he was carrying me off. Oh, not like a girl on a horse riding pillion ahead or behind as in the old stories, but rather like a leech on a sick person's body. I'd seen one of those when the Faerie Doctor came to cure Aunt Goldie's gout.

Curiouser and curiouser, as I'd learned long ago in *Alice's Adventures in Wonderland*, when I was still reading in the *A* section of the library. But it was likely a curiosity that was going to end badly. Especially if Wort continued to hold me that tight and run that fast through the darkness of the cave.

I was all but rocked to sleep by the constant motion, which was fine for the headache but not the rest of me, when of a sudden, Wort turned sharply and the cave suddenly seemed to take a steep, downward direction.

I was brought to full and fearful awareness by the sudden turn. What had I been thinking! What had I *not* been thinking? I was being as slow as Arian, without the gift of his sweetness and smile. It must have been because of my poor head, dull and achy. Or maybe I was still way too sick for this kind of adventure.

Or maybe this was all just a nightmare brought on by the ague. It was certainly odd enough to be one. *But if it is,* I thought, *it's a marvel of detail.* I'd never before had a dream that smelled.

At a guess, I was not just underground, I was *Under the Hill,* somewhere either in Seelie or Unseelie territory. Since no one in the Seelie Court, with their elegance and affectations (as Father had often enough described them), would pal around with something like Wort, I felt I knew where we were headed. And it wasn't a pleasant thought. If I was right, we were heading into the depths of the Unseelie Court, where they ate little Shouting Fey like me.

And while being eaten would certainly fix my headache, wing, and leg, it certainly wouldn't get me home in time for the christening or save my Family from bursting into a thousand stars. So I began to struggle, twisting and turning and shifting and wriggling.

All that did was give the McGargle permission to hold me even more tightly, which made me cry out in pain. The cry encouraged him to hold me all the closer, until it felt as if I were bound up with iron chains.

Stupid, stupid Gorse, I told myself. *And if you* had *gotten free—where would you go? You can't see in the dark. You'd probably run right into the nearest wall or another cave wort and still be delivered to the Unseelie Court.*

"Packaged for dinner." I spoke the words aloud, and they became true as soon as I said them. So, with that fearful notion embedded in my brain, I tried not to think anymore, lest I make it worse. Despite Father's often-repeated "Think, Gorse, think," I simply stopped all thought until the strange orange flames of a large hearth suddenly came into view. I promised myself then that thinking bad thoughts was something I'd never do again, if the Lords of Magick let me live. And that was a very big *if* indeed. But for some reason, the headache, at least, was gone, though the wing still hurt like stink, and now the burn on my leg felt hot and sore.

I kicked one foot at Wort. The one not attached to the burned leg. It was the only part of me I could move.

"Hey!" I said. "Slow down. Or put me down."

He did neither, just kept running toward the light, toward the hearth, toward what was surely the dinner fire. And there was nothing I could do to stop him.

Except . . .

Except . . .

Except Shout and hope it would work.

Now, I'd never attempted a Real Shout before. Just small ones.

Once I brought down a whole basket of apples from a tree too tall for me to climb and too crowded with fruit for me to fly into.

Another time I'd Shouted a snake out of a hole where a family of mice were cowering.

Of course I was technically still a child and had not been properly trained yet. Training starts on one's fourteenth birthday, and I was thirteen. However, I'd listened to Shouts all my life, heard the Aunts talk about how they were done. Eavesdropped and sneaked about enough when my brothers and sisters were learning. And Dusty told me all about his training. In those days, Dusty told me *everything*. So, I could only hope that this time I knew enough.

Not all of the Family actually have the gift, especially those of us with Father's blood coursing through our veins. Arian certainly has no Shout, and we're all lucky for that, because he'd have no control. Cambria, likewise, and her silliness is partially to blame. Bobbin and Robbin share the power but can hardly ever cooperate long enough to make it work. And I hadn't yet been trained, so no one—especially not me—knew if I'd a real talent for it or was, as Father put it, "only a dabbler."

Still, if ever there was a time for me to push out a Shout, the kind that comes on its own accord and is probably never repeated, this was the moment. Not apples, not mice this time, but my own life depended upon it.

So I drew in a deep breath, in between one bumpy Wort step and the next. Then I opened my mouth, and from the hollow spot down below my breastbone, what Great-aunt Gilda calls "the Sweetened Spot," I breathed out something big. Something enormous. I could feel it push into my throat, into my mouth, and rest for a moment on my tongue, where it felt hot as fever, cold as snow.

Then I gave that Shout one last push. It was, without doubt, the loudest sound I'd ever made in my life. Though of course just sound isn't enough. There's still timbre, temper, and tension, the Three *T*'s, as Great-aunt Gilda calls them. And each of them has to be just right.

At the same time there's the Wish. It has to be a rhymed Wish. That gives it the power. And I should have taken time to construct it well. But I had no time.

I thought as hard as I could about that Wish. I Wished . . . I Wished . . . that the fire, the hairy wort, and the Unseelie

Court would all go out at the same time, just as if an entire river had washed them all away.

Hairy monster, and your glare,
Be done, be gone, caught unaware,
Fire singe you, fire light you,
Fire ring you, fire fight you.

And to be extra sure, I pictured Wort in my mind, with a wildfire lighting up his entire hairy body.

The Shout whooshed out of me, burning my tongue, my lips. It felt as if I'd thrown up hot tea—not chamomile or mint, but something much stronger. Ginger tea, probably. The Shout echoed off the rock walls, off the rock floor, off the rock ceiling. It doubled back on itself, redoubling and trebling as it went. I shook with the Shout, exalted with it, felt as if I were floating on the sound of it. Burned with it.

Then, slowly, the Shout died away.

Wort was on fire and dropped me, and then he and the strange orange fire went out simultaneously.

Two out of three, I thought, *not bad for a first major try.*

Then I hit the floor with a thud, and I wondered if I'd go out, too, thinking, *This is getting to be a really* bad *habit.* But this time I managed to stay awake. Just. It was the pain in my right wing, banged again when I hit the ground, that kept me from fainting.

·7·

BOUND

After rolling around on the cold floor to try and assess my hurt wing, I managed to get up. The orange light had come back on again, so I shuffled toward it. I was careful to go slowly so as not to trip over anything—or anyone—this time, and hoped no one would see me.

The fire was seductive, and I was so cold, I curled up by it to get warm. The warmth seemed to soothe my head and seep into my hurt wing as well, so I shut my eyes—not to sleep, but to let the fire work its small magick on my battered body. But I kept alert for any sound of someone—or something—trying to sneak up on me.

I woke still lying by the fire with my arms bound behind me, both Cloak and spindle gone, and a bright light in my face from a globe worm held in a massive hand. Not a massive hairy hand like Wort's, but a massive leather-gloved hand.

"It lives," someone remarked with neither kindness nor care at the core, only a lingering weariness, as if he were too tired to say anything else. Then he spat out two more brief words. "Now what?"

Another voice, drier than the first, with a hint of cold laughter behind it, said, "We ask its name and then we eat it."

"If you ask my name," I said with a bravado I hardly felt, "and I give it, you can't possibly eat me. It wouldn't be polite. Pudding—Alice."

"Pudding Alice," said the first voice. "What kind of a fey name is that?"

Silently, I vowed to say no more. I'd meant Pudding Alice as a reference to *Through the Looking-Glass*, the second book about Alice, where Alice and the Pudding are introduced and then she, being a polite child, knows she couldn't possibly eat something or some*one* she'd just met. Clearly these two world-weary men had never read the book. Or possibly *any* book. Fey rarely do read, as the Family proved. And if, as I suspected, these were Unseelie, they would be the least likely of all fey to find enjoyment there.

So, if these two wanted Pudding Alice to be my true name, it would slow down any magick they might try on me.

Or so I hoped.

"Politeness," said the dry voice, now almost smothered in laughter, "has never been a part of my makeup."

"Unseelie," I said, totally forgetting my vow of silence. Luckily I hadn't made the vow an Oath by speaking it aloud, or I would have been bursting into stars at that very moment. "Dry, unfeeling, they hold little sacred."

"Shouting Fey—silly, useless, powerless misfits," the voice behind the globe worm countered. "*And* you've been tutored by elves."

"By my Father." I sat up too quickly, which made my head spin, and the ache from the residue of my Shout and the Unseelie Court's stone walls returned. I was suddenly aware that the place was throbbing with magick. And my headache wasn't helped by the fact that I was now also terrified I'd already given too much away.

The globe worm was lowered just enough so I could see behind to the fey eyes that now crinkled with humor. I wondered why. Father never mentioned that the Unseelie folk had a sense of humor, only a hot anger that burned them dry from the inside out, until they were only walking husks.

"Finn's Get?" the distant Dry Voice hazarded.

"Close," I answered, thinking of Uncle Finn, whom I'd never met and now probably never would. It seemed silly to hide the connection. And it hurt my head too much to try. The Unseelie might torture me otherwise and find out the same thing, so why not tell this interrogator right out? Surely he could see I was only a child. That might soften him a bit. "My Uncle."

Just as I had that thought, he moved close and laughed full in my face.

"An elven *child* is as dangerous as a full-grown one. And a damned Shouter!"

Really? I thought. *Me, dangerous?* That hardly seemed likely. But I decided to let him think that. It could be useful. Or dangerous. I decided to go with useful.

The one holding the globe worm set it onto a rock jut and the worm crawled away, but the glow it had given off still wavered around us. I'd no idea how long that glow would last. *A minute? An hour?*

But in that lingering light, I looked more closely at the man with the dry voice, who was clearly the leader of the two. Father always says that knowledge will set us free, which is why he reads so many books. Though from what he'd told me about our being tied to the land, knowledge hadn't actually freed any of us yet. Still, I thought it best to assume that it could help me somehow with these most recent bonds, those holding my arms behind my back. I'd nothing better to hope with anyway. So I looked directly at my captor but tried at the same time to seem totally disinterested in anything he had to say.

Dry Voice was most certainly a princeling. Maybe even a king. Both his stature and clothing argued for it. His strong face bones were almost elfin in their sharpness. His shining eyes, yellow in the fading light, were cat's-eye bright. Tight leather trews and high boots set off his legs, and a leather jerkin over a bloodred blouse lent him the appearance of a long-legged insect. *A handsome, long-legged insect.* The pin on his shoulder probably signified his house or class or rank, though I'd never seen one before except in a book. The pin bore a crest that looked something like a flying dragon, something like a dragonfly. As I watched, his hands folded together as if in a prayer, but that was probably just a show of confidence. His thumbs beat against each other. He wasn't frightened of me one bit.

But he scared the sweetness out of me!

"Shouter indeed," I said. "But I don't think we're damned." I smiled slowly at him to show a confidence I didn't really have. Headaches do that to me. "Only exiled. In the Light. Above the Hill." It was fine to tell him this. He'd already guessed it.

"That's not what some of our other . . . visitors . . . have told us. They have had a different slant."

That's when he smiled back. It wasn't a comforting smile, but it didn't frighten me further. Perhaps like certain great witches, Prince Dry Voice *liked* feisty children. Perhaps he even liked Shouting girls. Though if that were so, he'd much prefer Solange, who is the great beauty of our Family. Or perhaps he was just thinking of a private joke. Or an old pain he disguised with a sinister smile.

Or perhaps, I thought suddenly and shivered, he was remembering a recipe for cooked Gorse.

"Pudding Alice," he said, "I have a proposition for you."

I nodded. A proposition could put off dinner for long enough. Long enough for me to figure out a way to get free. At least so I hoped.

"I'm listening," I said carefully.

"You will listen more closely with your hands unbound," he said, which was certainly true. He signaled to his leather-gloved underling.

"Majesty." The henchman's voice was full of warning.

Prince Dry Voice ignored the warning and laughed. It was a real laugh, not a sinister one this time. His laugh was handsome, too, in an insecty kind of way.

"Child," he said, directing all his considerable charm at me, "I am *sure* you are listening. It delays dinner." Then he turned to the henchman. "Grey, where's Gargle? I want to congratulate him for catching this little elven princess. I want her to see him in the light. After all, she may be just what we need, and if she sees Gargle, she may become more . . ." He looked for the word, then suddenly found it: "Cooperative."

He was exaggerating, of course. I was no more an elven princess than . . . than I was a full-breed elf. It must have been Solange's old dress, sparkling in the globe worm's light, that had given him that impression, even with a patch missing from the tumble down into the faerie trap. But I wasn't about to give him a reason to change his mind. Maybe Unseelie princes didn't eat princesses.

And then I had a wonderful thought: *I have two names: Grey, the second in command. And Gargle.* Gargle. *The creature had simply been telling me his name.* A cold tremor ran up my backbone. Now that I had the furry Wort's real name, I was deeply ashamed. Pudding, meet Alice. *I killed him.* The tremor crossed between my shoulder blades. *I've never killed* anything *before.*

I didn't have any shame about Grey. I hadn't Shouted at him.

Yet.

"I haven't seen Gargle since that great flare of fire, my lord," Grey said in his weary voice. The voice didn't match his looks. Slightly younger than the prince, he worked hard at looking stronger. But there were laugh lines at his temples, and his hair was the same as Dusty's—golden, flyaway curls. He sported a small golden beard. His clothes were simpler than the prince's—a gray silken shirt, a leather doublet, tight trews. Nothing at all like what my brothers wore.

The Unseelie prince noticed me trembling and stared at me for a moment. "Pudding Alice, what *are* you?"

I stared at him, not understanding the question.

"Was it *you* made that flare and disappeared Gargle, my good and faithful cave troll? His family will not be happy with you, not happy at all."

He has a family*?*

The shame deepened. I had no answer. The best route all along had been to say nothing. Of course, saying nothing was not exactly my greatest strength. But now it was imperative that I try.

I smiled weakly.

"Untie her," Prince Dry Voice said to Grey.

"But, my lord, she's dangerous."

"*She's* not dangerous. But her mouth is," the prince replied.

Grey shook his head, and at the same time tried to look as if he wasn't shaking his head. "Then shouldn't we gag her?"

At that, the Unseelie prince broke into a full laugh before turning and addressing me. "Sometimes I wonder if

I am always to be surrounded by idiots and incompetents. Should I tell him or will you?"

I hadn't a notion as to what he meant. Besides, I was doing my best to remain silent. So I bowed my head like a princess advising a prince.

He took that to mean he was to tell his hireling himself. He leaned toward Grey. "A Shouting Fey can speak through cloth, through wood, through stone," he said. "The only way to stop her would be to cut off her head."

I looked down at the floor, blinking furiously. Why had no one ever told *me* that? And as an afterthought, I wondered, *Is it true? Is the Shout* that *powerful?* I supposed I would have found out on my fourteenth birthday, when my tutorial in Shouting began. But I doubted now I'd ever have that chance. My eyes began to fill with tears, and I looked steadily at the floor until I was sure I wouldn't weep.

When I looked up again, ready to ask the inevitable question, Grey was already drawing his sword from its sheath.

"As you wish, my lord," he said. His handsome face gave nothing away, not anger, not fear, not eagerness to cut off my head. The perfect soldier.

I gritted my teeth, willing myself to be strong and not to faint. My head began to ache furiously and there was something throbbing in my right temple. If Grey brought that large blade down on my small neck, losing my head shouldn't hurt for long. Or at least I hoped so. And at least it would stop the headache. Too bad I no longer had the Cloak and couldn't go invisible. *If* it worked. It didn't appear to be all that predictable.

Appear. Cloak of Invisibility. I'd made a joke right before dying, with no one to tell it to.

Good-bye, Mother; good-bye, Father, I thought, and began to go down the long list of brothers, sisters, cousins, Aunts, and my Great-aunt, all of whom would surely miss me. Being dead, I couldn't very well miss them. Or tell them my Will, not that I had much to give away.

In sudden misery, I thought of all the books I'd never read, all the stories I'd never hear. How I'd never told Mother I loved her.

Then, just as suddenly I stopped my mental babble, found my courage, and gave myself a kind of mental slap across the face. I opened my mouth, and prepared to give a *really* loud Shout to put both of these Unseelie men out, remembering just in time that we only get one Shout per day, and I'd already used up mine.

·8·
THE PROPOSITION

Think, Gorse, think! I heard Father's voice in my head. So I bit my lower lip and really tried to figure things out.

Why, I thought, *would an actual Unseelie prince be living in a cave?*

I answered myself: *He's Under the Hill.*

But surely—I continued thinking—*Under the Hill is supposed to be a metaphor. A fanciful statement meaning another realm, hard to find, difficult to get into. Not—you know—an actual* cave.

I looked around in the lowering light. Stone walls. Stone floors. Stone ceiling with stone pillars dropping down and stone pillars flowing up from the floor.

Clearly and unmistakably a cave. I'd seen pictures of them in a book about caves, in the *C* section of the library.

So I was right back to the original question. *Why would an actual Unseelie prince be in an* actual *cave?*

I gave it more thought. On the one hand, Prince Dry Voice was probably wicked enough to have been sent into exile. His second in command certainly seemed awfully ready to take heads off at the prince's whim.

On the other hand, the prince was handsome enough for love, unrequited or otherwise. *Maybe,* I thought, *he tried to steal another Unseelie prince's wife.* I liked that. Made him both sneaky *and* romantic.

I smiled. Then I worried that I was trying to make Dry Voice a hero and not the villain that he surely was, trapping girls who belonged to a different court and hauling them below ground.

And what about those "visitors" who told him about the Shouters? Could they have been the Uncles? Were they actual *visitors or had they fallen in through a magick trap just like me? And—another awful thought—had they told the prince everything over a cup of tea? Or at a dinner, after which they were the main course?*

So there I was, stuck somewhere between admiring Prince Dry Voice and fearing him, liking him and hating him. I was getting no closer to the answers.

• • • • • • • •

Also, I was no closer to finding either the dropped Cloak of Invisibility or the spindle.

Or discovering a way out of the cave.

Or—

Suddenly, interrupting the cascade of my thoughts, a hundred globe worms lit the cavern. The fire was once again flaming in the hearth. No matter how much I feared Grey's sword, the prince was certainly efficient.

Now I could see clearly that the cavern was no simple cave, but rather a great chamber, draped with elegant tapestries, all of which seemed to depict hunting scenes. In one, fey hunters, their golden hair pulled back in mare's tails, sighted down long bows at fanciful beasts that had too many horns, or too few legs. Some of the beasts ran crouched over, and some ran upright. In another tapestry, the size of a coverlet, a collared unicorn lay imprisoned within a small white fence. It reminded me of something I'd seen before but couldn't actually name. In a third, vicious dogs savaged the unicorn that lay meekly bleeding, while its blood dripped over the edge of the tapestry, dangling there, seemingly ready to drop onto the cave floor.

I turned my head and saw tables I hadn't noticed before, groaning with food: boned and deboned meat of cattle and lambs, three kinds of fowl, sitting on golden platters; breads in seven sizes from tiny muffins to long, twisted loaves lay in willow baskets; green salads and gold salads and salads made with vegetables dyed all colors of the rainbow overflowed pottery bowls. Though how the prince and his obviously fine chef knew about rainbows stuck down here was something I couldn't explain. I couldn't imagine at that moment where they could have found cows and lambs either.

On one enormous plank of polished wood lay stuffed fish with their tails in their mouths; on another, ice dishes were aflame with peppers and flowers. Flagons decorated with jewel-encrusted dragons sat brimful with something red and sparkling that I hoped was wine. Or grape juice. Or even the squeezings of beetroot.

There was an entire table holding cakes and puddings, from deep dark chocolate of the forests to the light, white coconut meat of the desert isles. Not that I'd ever had any deep dark chocolate or white coconut, though I'd read accounts of them and seen pictures in the books on food in the *C* section of the library: Cookbooks and Culinary. My mouth filled with desire and drool.

I was enchanted by it all. Hunger imprisoned me far more efficiently than had the handsome henchman.

Suddenly, I heard a wisp of a fiddle followed immediately by the high keening of a pipe. Both fiddler and piper appeared, dressed in motley like fools, dancing to their own tunes. They were followed quickly by three young tumblers, who leaped and somersaulted after them, the stone floor making no difference to their acrobatics, for they never missed a step and were so graceful, I couldn't hear a single footfall.

Finally, in came what could only have been the Unseelie Court itself: fey men and women in full regalia, wings tipped with blinking lights. They were dressed for a grand ball, that much was certain, for all had lace at the neck, bodices of green and gold, and proper masks with the exaggerated features of gargoyles. Great-aunt Gilda had often regaled us with stories about masked balls where princes fell in love with masked ladies, stories her Mother had told her. These fey folk looked just like the ones in the tales.

In marched the courtiers in time to the fiddle and pipe, laughing behind their hands, gossiping, looking not at all different from how Fergus and Banshee must have looked in their prime, judging from the paintings hanging in Great-aunt Gilda's hall. Or like Solange, Darna, and Willow when they played dress-up in the Aunts' old gowns. But I had never seen such sumptuousness, such elegance, such beauty. Suddenly our ratty belvederes, our tatty pavilions and follies, our hand-me-down clothing, our small, homey picnics seemed threadbare and embarrassing.

The courtiers drew themselves into a circle that encompassed the entire Great Hall and slowly began to dance. Their laughter only ceased when they performed the strict figures of a pavane, as if a somber face were needed to accomplish the difficult steps. Or perhaps they were simply counting the beats as they went, as my brothers and sisters and I had done when Great-aunt Gilda taught us the dance. Except for Dusty, of course, who just threw himself into any activity with vigor.

"Instead of rigor," as Great-aunt Gilda always said of Dusty's dancing, with a sniff.

Whatever the reason, the courtiers danced with little grace and less joy. Unseelie to the core, I guessed.

There was a small bit of movement at the edge of my vision, so I turned my head. Prince Dry Voice was now sitting on a high throne I hadn't seen before, and at his right hand was Grey, *his* hand on the great sword with which he'd volunteered to take my head off. I was sure it had been the movement of that hand to that sword that had caught my attention. Neither of them were looking at the dancers, but at me.

Suddenly I wondered at the party and the partiers. They were too beautiful, too perfect. Immediately, I thought, *Is it a glamour, all these lords and ladies of the Unseelie Court?* I wanted desperately for it to be real. Especially the food.

But suddenly I gaped at the dancers, at the tables, at

everything, trying to grasp the truth. *Probably,* I thought, *they're really only enchanted rats and bats and moles. Or Gargle's family.* And then an even twistier idea came to me: *Perhaps it's the dark cave that's the* real *glamour.*

I shook my head. *How am I to know? How will I* ever *know?*

The prince rose from his throne and held out his hand to me. I'd no choice but to take it. His hand was as cool and dry as his voice.

"You must be hungry, Pudding Alice," he said. "Let us eat." And he led me to the groaning tables.

As we crossed the space, I smelled something that was neither sweet nor savory, and was certainly not food. Rather the smell was cool, earthy, herbal, slightly sour, almost damp.

A cave smell. I reached out and brushed my fingertips across a waterfall of stone that grew down from the roof. At once, I remembered what such a thing was called: *Stalactite.* It had been in the book about caves.

I knew then that there wasn't any food there for me, not *real* food, because it had no smell. Only the cave had a smell. As Father used to say, talking about glamours, "Your eyes and ears will lie to you, but smells never lie. Trust the smell." My stomach growled out a warning, because faerie food—if it's glamoured—is dangerous to eat, even for us fey. Eating such fare makes you forget who you are and what your mission. It changes, even stops time. Or, as Father had once explained, it doesn't so much change time as change one's *perception* of time.

"I'm not hungry," I said. "Not hungry for *that* food, anyway."

"I wonder why it has taken you this long to figure that out," Dry Voice answered, and we both knew that he didn't just mean the food. He meant the glamour. He waved his hand in the direction of the dancers, musicians, and tables of food. They disappeared at once.

"Majesty . . ." It was Grey at his side. I didn't need to look to know his hand was on his sword. His hand was *always* on his sword.

"She will not Shout at us, even though she knows," the prince countered. "We now understand each other, *Pudding Alice* and I." He spoke the name, Pudding Alice, with a certain quiet irony to let me know that he'd known all along it wasn't my true name.

But I was more interested in the other thing he'd said, and started to think—*really think*—about that.

He'd said, "We now understand each other."

Understand what?

Maybe he meant I understood about the glamour. But then I realized that I was *really* thinking about the fact that

Prince Dry Voice didn't seem to know I only had one Shout in me till another day ticked over. He didn't seem to know that *none* of the Shouting Fey could give more than one Shout a day. And how could he, if Fergus and Banshee had left the faerie courts before they'd had children who were the start of the Shouters? And maybe he ate the Uncles before they told him all they knew about us.

I shuddered.

Perhaps the Uncles hadn't actually known about the once-a-day Shouts. After all, which Aunt would have ever let out that bit of information to a mere human? Gardenia? Never! Glade? Grania? Goldie? It was unthinkable any of them would tell the secrets of our magick to anyone not of the Family. And *I* wasn't about to let Dry Voice, an *Unseelie* prince, know. The threat of a Shout was worth a lot to me. Let him think I could Shout all day and all night long. It made things almost even.

Almost.

"Understanding," I said thoughtfully, "is easy to get and easier to lose." It was something Father had once said to Dusty when he'd been sent to the library by Mother for a telling-off. Pretending to be asleep among the books, I'd heard Father's soft, thoughtful voice as he scolded Dusty, but I had never understood what he'd meant until now.

The prince chuckled, and *his* voice was like wind over the last of the harvestable corn. "Now leave us alone, Grey. You breathe in conspiracies and breathe out venom. I will not have our little princess envapored with such air while we deepen our understanding."

Grey left us, but only so far as beyond the direct light of a taper set in a deep sconce anchored into the cave wall. I could no longer see *him*, but his shadow arm on his shadow sword was still visible, and I didn't forget for a moment that he was close by. I knew him now, had read about his kind. He could edge into a room, and no one would see him, almost as if he had a Cloak like Banshee's. But if you looked for his shadow, he was always there.

The prince took me by the elbow and steered me toward the hearth. He tried to act companionably, but there was steel in his grip. That grip said plainly that he was in control and I was not to run away—even though we both knew I'd nowhere to run to. He guided me firmly toward a small stone table near the hearth where two chairs sat close together, legs under the table, as if for warmth. Pulling one of the chairs out, he gestured for me to sit down.

Suddenly feeling as if all that I'd been through in the past few hours was sinking heavily down the insides of my legs, I was more than willing to sit. I was so tired, I might have even fallen asleep where I stood. But once I sat, the danger of sleep would loom even greater. And I needed to think about my plans.

Luckily, the prince gave me little time to nod off. He had much more to say to me.

"So—here," he began, "is my proposition, Pudding Alice. As you have guessed, I cannot leave this cave, this dungeon, that has been my home for more years than I can count. Nor can Grey, who came willingly with me, my ally, my cousin, my good right hand. We have been Cursed to remain in this place."

I hadn't guessed *any* of that, except that Grey was certainly the prince's good right hand. However, the information that Grey was also Dry Voice's cousin was very interesting indeed. So I nodded and let the prince think what he liked.

"Why don't you just fly out?" I said.

He laughed sourly. "We have been triply Cursed, child. To stay here and to become wingless are two. The third is that any magick traps we have made work only one way. You cannot fly out, only in."

I think my mouth gaped. To be Cursed once might be an accident. To be Cursed twice was certainly done with huge malice. To be Cursed a third time . . . well, if he meant me to feel sorry for him, he'd done a really good job. *If* he was telling the truth. But why had they been imprisoned? And did that make him more to be feared—or less?

"I have to stay here," he told me, "but *you* can leave, child. And I will show you how. However, you must first vow to do me one small thing before you go back into the Light." He said it with a guileless smile, as if swearing a vow was of no real consequence, just a few words, hand over the heart, fingers crossed in the game sign.

I was suddenly back to not trusting him. Did he *truly* believe the Shouting Fey were so stupid, we'd no knowledge of what a spoken vow was? It was a solemn Oath. And I knew all about Oaths and Biddings. After Father had stopped Necrops from making Carnell swear, Great-aunt Gilda had stepped in. A stickler for the Old Ways, she taught us all she knew about Oath-taking, swearing, vows, and magick. We were well schooled in that, my brothers, sisters, cousins, and I. I was not yet up on everything I needed to know about Shouting, but about Oaths, I certainly knew the consequences of breaking them.

But then I had another thought. Perhaps this awful Dry Voice prince simply didn't care what I did or didn't know. He just wanted me to swear without telling me what the Oath was about.

If I gave him my Oath, it would be unbreakable. If I didn't do what I swore to, I'd burst into a thousand stars—like motes of sunlight—and be gone.

For a moment, I thought of poor, young Goldenrod, the fey Uncle I'd never known, becoming motes of light on the path. I shivered, and not with the cold. If I swore the Oath and then failed to do his Bidding, the only thing that would save me from such a fate would be the death of the Oath-maker before me, and he, that crafty prince, looked very much alive.

No, I didn't trust him at all now.

If I burst apart into a thousand stars, I'd never see Father or Mother or any of my brothers or sisters, not to mention the Aunts and all the cousins ever again. Though I wasn't sure never seeing whiny, whey-faced Mallow again would be a burden. I still had time, I hoped, to get back to the christening. But if I burst into stars here, I'd put them all in horrible danger besides. Or maybe not. If I ceased to exist, maybe the Bidding by the king couldn't include me and the Family would be saved.

Oh, it was a puzzle.

But, I thought, *what if Prince Dry Voice's Bidding is unspeakable? Unconscionable? What if it's something that benefits only an Unseelie lord, not a thirteen-year-old daughter of the Shouting Fey?* There were lots of things the prince might ask me to do that I couldn't do. I couldn't murder someone for him. I couldn't cheat someone in his name. I couldn't hurt a child. Or a dog, for that matter. Though snakes . . . well, I *could* hurt snakes if I had to.

The problem with that kind of horrible thinking is that once you start, it's hard to stop.

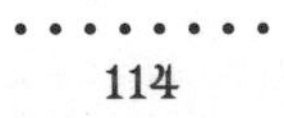

I went round and round in my head on this, and my eyelids started trembling with unshed tears. My fingers twitched. I had so many *ifs* and *buts* and *howevers* and *mights*, I could hardly breathe, hardly remember them all.

Then, at the lowest part of my thoughts, came this notion: *If he wants me to do something terrible, I could always* choose *to burst into those thousand stars. That would be the heroic thing to do. Though, of course, Father would never know that I'd been a hero. And Mother and the Aunts would never know I'd mastered the Shout, the one that killed Gargle.*

So then I began to mourn Gargle, who was simply carrying me carefully to his master. Had made no threats to me. Had not otherwise harmed me. And I'd murdered him with a calculated Shout.

That was it! *A Shout!* How could I have been so stupid, so thick? Not even fear or anger or exhaustion was an excuse.

I could beg for time, could *bargain* for time, could ask to sleep on the decision. In the morning, when I'd have a new chance at another Shout, I could gather my strength, Shout—and get rid of the prince *and* his henchman Grey. I'd figure a way out of the cave and—

Oh, the Curse of thinking too much! Father had always urged me to think, but this was overmuch, because suddenly I had the worst thought of all: *The Shout hadn't affected the Unseelie pair before, and surely they'd been close enough when I*

Shouted poor Gargle into an early grave. Yes, the Shout had been Wort specific, but it had been my first Great Shout ever, and surely there would have been leaks all around the edges. Even when the Aunts Shouted, leakage was a problem. Something Father called "collateral damage," a phrase from one of the books on human wars that he had read.

So I gave this problem careful thought: *The prince and Grey seem entirely untouched by the Shout that killed poor Gargle. If I give a Shout tomorrow and it bothers neither of them, Grey will surely cut off my head, and that wouldn't be half as epic or heroic as bursting into a thousand stars. And—*

And then, all unaccountably, I began to weep and couldn't stop. I wept from exhaustion and fear, my nose running so with snot that I had to wipe it away with the corner of my skirt. Well, Solange's skirt.

So much for heroism.

So much for begging for time.

The prince turned away in disgust and called out, "Grey, come here!"

And Grey—his hand on his sword and the sword already halfway out of its sheath—left his shadow and came at the prince's call.

"Tell her," the prince commanded, either moved by my tears, or embarrassed, or disgusted. It was hard to tell.

"My lord?" Hand still on sword, no longer a shadow, Grey looked puzzled.

"Tell her my story." The prince's voice sounded defeated. No, not defeated, just infinitely tired and suddenly old.

Grey nodded, but only a finger-width's worth. If I hadn't been staring fixedly at him, I might not have noticed.

He turned his back on the prince and looked right at me and began.

"This is the tale of the Unseelie Prince Orybon the Recluded, the shut-away. Orybon the Restless, sometimes mistranslated by his enemies as 'the Reckless,' but he was never such a one. And he is now occasionally called by me 'the Recluse.' He was, in fact, the firstborn of the mighty King Oberon and Queen Mab and—"

"Do not add all your footnotes and furbelows," the prince said tetchily. "Just tell it plain. She is a child, not a professor at the university."

Grey nodded again; this time a tiny smile seemed to play around his lips. The first I'd seen from him, though it might simply have been a trick of the candlelight. It changed his face, softened it for a moment. He continued.

"Orybon was from birth pledged to the Seelie princess Maeve and—as was the custom among royals of the day—she was sent to live in his parents' castle, where he was to become her friend long before he was to become her wedded lord. A quaint custom and much abused amongst the upper classes of the Unseelie Court, but not by us."

I wondered what "us" he meant. The royal family? Or just Prince Orybon and himself? Perhaps it was what Father called "claiming the high ground" whenever my sisters started squabbling and I was about to join in. But as I said nothing of this aloud, Grey continued, though he looked at me oddly, almost as if he could read my thoughts.

"And so it happened," he said, turning slightly away from me, "that Ory and May, as they called one another, became fast friends. They fished in the ponds together for golden trout, plaited willow wands into hoops, which she twined with ribands, and read together by the hearth fire such works as the roundels of the poet Oviticus, and the hero tales of Anwyn and Astrodel and . . ."

For a moment I stopped listening and considered this. If they had willow wands and fished in ponds, they had to be living above ground, not below. Or at least they had to have access to the up above. I must have made a quick intake of breath at this revelation, because Grey had turned back to stare at me.

But the prince had also moved, rather uneasily, in his chair, then leaned forward and glared at Grey. "Now you are condescending to her. Telling her faerie tales. We didn't read to one another, certainly not poncy poetry. Pudding

Alice is not a baby. She is, by the gods, a princess of the fey. Literate by the sound of her speech, and smart, too. Just . . . get . . . on . . . with it!" He spoke the last as if his teeth had snapped together and he had to push the words out through them, which took a lot of effort.

I didn't bother to show by even the slightest twitch of my lips how funny I thought their quarreling was. However, while they were picking at each other, they weren't picking on me. Besides, I was actually enjoying the story the way Grey told it, both the professorial footnotes and the references to childish things, not that I was going to tell either one of them that. The story was incredibly romantic, too, just as I thought it might be. Besides, I was learning a lot more about both men as the telling went on.

Grey bowed, though it looked suspiciously as if he were mocking the prince.

Mocking him?

Suddenly I realized that these two had been imprisoned together for so many years, any family love had turned to stone, much as the walls around them. They'd become each other's bonds, burdens, scapegoats. They hated each other even while professing love. They would do anything to win free of the cave—and each other. And here I was, not really a girl or a princess or anything else to them except the hope of, and the possible means of, their final escape.

Just as my Aunts and Mother had at one time thought me to be the One to solve their great problem, so now did Prince Orybon and Grey.

Think, Gorse, think! I had realized the most important thing of all: the two princes needed me as much as I needed them. *Or more!* And I'd only have their trust as long as they believed that I could effect their escape. So I knew that I had to feign interest, whether I had any or not.

Just listen, I reminded myself. Everything I learned about them would be something more that might eventually be of use in my *own* escape, whether it was to be by climbing the stone walls, flying away through the stone corridors once my wing healed, or killing them both with a Shout. Possibly a combination of all three.

I could almost hear Father's voice saying, "Well thought out, Gorse," and so congratulating myself, I managed to miss the next sentence or two of Grey's tale. I only hoped they hadn't been important sentences, only more footnotes and furbelows, whatever those were.

"Maeve," Grey was saying, "had been a lovely child and grew into an even lovelier woman with white-gold hair, porcelain skin, and a voice that sounded like larks ascending into the dawn.

"Orybon, on the other hand, grew into his one great gift, the gift of True Cursing. He began with Curses that lasted an hour, then a day, a week, a month, a year. He practiced on roses, butterflies, brachet hounds; he tried them out on serving wenches, changelings, even a fifth cousin or two. But discreetly, always discreetly. Until, by his twentieth year, he had become quite proficient at the Making and Directing of Cursing, though not—I hasten to add—at love."

"Do not hasten on my account," said the prince.

"But I do *everything* on your account," said Grey. "And without recompense, as you know."

I wanted to ask what *recompense* was. I wanted to know what Maeve thought of her friend's gift. I wanted to know what kind of Curses the prince made. Were they simple Transformations, such as boy into bird, that ended by morning? Were they Malform Wishes: such as a nose like a turkey's? Were they Generational Gestures: one's family would henceforth all be born with webbed fingers and toes? Were they Curses only against the fey, or were some against humans? Would they put someone to sleep for a hundred years or bury them deep beneath the earth or send them to the moon? And most important—did the Curses last?

But I didn't dare interrupt the flow of the story. If I did, I might get Cursed by Orybon himself, for that—I now knew—was Prince Dry Voice's true name.

Grey had already restarted the story, hardly slowed by his cousin's interruptions or my silent speculations.

"In fact, Orybon became so enraptured by Cursing, he paid too little attention to the ever-lovely Maeve, growing apace into her great beauty, and, in that way, ended up becoming Cursed himself. For women like to be wooed and won, not taken for granted and married as a matter of course."

"That much is false, cousin. Besides, what do you know of love and marriage, you would-be priest, you voluntary oblate, you dried-up raisin? If we were not between these Cursed stone walls, I would have you changed into a centipede in no time." Prince Orybon's whisper grated with anger, and he stood and began to pace.

I didn't show for an instant what I'd just heard and understood. Not a twitch. But I trembled with excitement. That the prince could do glamours down in the cave, that much I already knew. *But no other magick!* It was an odd thought. The cave, evidently, could augment some magick, like my Shout. And dampen down other things. And the whole place throbbed with Old Magick, reeked of it—though evidently not his. I had to think about that. I was careful not to smile, but from that moment on, I sharpened my listening skills.

Grey had shrugged off his cousin's poisonous name-calling easily, and simply went on with the telling of the story.

"The princess turned instead to Orybon's younger brother, the not quite so handsome but always attentive Lord Fergus. There was even a youngest brother, but he was of no account in the story since he'd already been exchanged for the youngest Seelie prince—me—and now resided in the Seelie Court, as I did in the Unseelie . . ."

I stopped listening and thought frantically: *Fergus? Is Fergus an ordinary name amongst the Highborns? And is, perhaps, Maeve really Banshee's true name?* I think my jaw dropped, so I quickly put my hand to my chin to disguise my surprise, pretending to yawn. But all the while I was thinking, *Is this, then, a story about the creation of the Shouting Fey? Were we once all Unseelie folk?* I shuddered, then thought, *Is this why Prince Orybon needs a Shouter to help him? Someone from his own Family?* I shuddered again thinking this, but I had to face facts. If Grey's story was true, Prince Orybon was my Great-grand-uncle, which made him the only true blood Uncle I'd ever known.

I no longer tried to remain still, unemotional, unreadable. In fact I was suddenly like a dog on point, my attention fully caught by the tale. I didn't even care if the prince or Grey noticed me noticing, as I leaned toward Grey to encourage his telling.

He went on, seemingly without noticing me at all, his fingers now laced together and his eyes on his hands.

"They met, Fergus and Maeve, in hallways on their way

to one room or another, on the castle allure gazing at the stars, sitting in the Great Hall and passing pleasantries, wandering down country lanes under the bending trees. She played her lute and sang in that glorious voice, and Fergus applauded. He always applauded. He did not disguise his obsession with her.

"All the while, Orybon was practicing his Curses—on honeybees and walnut trees; on sheep in sheepcotes and cattle in the field; on shepherdesses, milkmaids, even a page boy or two.

"One day, Orybon came upon his intended, Maeve, and his brother Fergus strolling in the arbor where the pungent dark grapes were all but bursting their skins. Fergus and Maeve had clearly just exchanged a first kiss and were still stunned by the heat of it."

"They had *not* kissed!" Orybon turned and roared. It was an awful sound. Then in a quieter voice, he added, "They may have been about to."

Grey houghed through his nose like a horse and looked up at the prince. "You do not know what had come before, cousin. The kiss you interrupted may have been a second kiss. Or a third. It may have included an embrace. A tongue. A promise. A . . ."

It was clearly an old argument between them. I left them to it, heading for the fire, and thinking, *Oh, Great-grandfather Fergus, what you have loosed . . . ?*

Seething in their individual anger over something that had happened so far in the past neither one of them could ever know the truth of it, the cousins looked away from one another. The story each told himself over and over had become more real than what had actually happened. I wondered idly why Orybon hadn't given me his own version without Grey's, and then realized that it was more important for him to needle Grey this way than simply tell me the tale as he remembered it.

That made me ask myself, Had I ever been so obstinate and ornery with my own Family? I'd certainly never been very attentive, hiding away in the library and reading books instead of having little more than the politest of conversations. Or hurrying away to my disguised meadow to be out of earshot of their tiffs. But I *never* would have Cursed them. Not even if that had been my one true gift.

Family, Father always said, *is what is left when everything else is gone.*

So I waited the cousins out, and finally Grey began again. So I returned to listen and watch him tell the tale.

"When Orybon saw the way the two looked at each other, he knew all that he had to know. He forgot about Cursing honeybees and walnut trees and the like. Raising his right hand, he spoke in a voice that was low but not at all careful."

The prince interrupted. "I am *always* careful."

Grey looked at him, smiled slowly, then looked at me. "Make up your own mind, Pudding," he said. "This is what the *careful* Prince Orybon said in his Curse:

"'Your greatest gift, woman,
shall be your special Curse.
'Twill put neither friendship nor money in your purse.
If he can still adore you as you sing him to his death,
You'll find that he will Curse you
with his final, final breath.'"

It was certainly a Curse that had lasted for centuries, though I didn't think much of Orybon's rhymes, probably because the Under the Hill fey back then had already been losing their ability to make spells in rhyme. Great-aunt Gilda's spell lyrics were certainly more elegant. Aunt Galda's more direct. And Aunt Gardenia's a lot more singable. Still, I had to admit that Prince Orybon's Curse, whatever its rhythmic flaws, had worked, because May became Banshee, and that Curse must have been what sent her off into the world Above the Hill with Fergus, where they had their daughters, one of whom became my Great-aunt Gilda and another who my Grandmother and . . .

It was like a mystery tale you solve long before the teller gets to that part of the plot. Banshee's greatest gift, her voice, became her Curse. Yet what the prince didn't know then—and probably wouldn't believe now—was that Fergus loved her anyway, and married her, and somehow they were exiled or left on their own and lived Above the Hill, though I'd never heard that Fergus Cursed Banshee as he lay dying, but perhaps he had. We Shouters tend to forget the bad stuff and dwell in what *might* be rather than what *is.* I guess that's why I wasn't told about being tied to the land till I was over thirteen. There's a poet whose book I read, in the *D*'s, who said something about that. "I dwell in Possibility—" she wrote, almost as if she were fey. And maybe she was.

So what Grey's story told me was that we Shouting Fey came because Prince Orybon Cursed his younger brother Fergus and his intended bride, Maeve. And the only other living witness to what had happened after that was this Prince Grey, from the Seelie Court, brought to the Unseelie Court as a hostage prince.

So was it really a Curse?

Or a Blessing?

Or both?

Whichever, here was me in the middle, puzzling it all out.

But Grey was still telling the tale, so I stopped thinking and once again listened with care.

"Then," Grey said, "Orybon turned on his heel and was

gone from them, not wanting to watch their faces—once so full of the heat of their love—melt like candle wax in the greater heat of his Curse."

The good thing about the story was that it was clear I knew more about Fergus and Banshee than the two of them did. The bad thing was that they knew much more about the other Curse, the one that sent them into the cave prison, than I did. And either they wouldn't—or couldn't—tell me more until I swore the Oath.

The Oath.

It always came back to that.

9

TELLING LIES

"So, girl," Prince Orybon said, his voice like the sound of a lizard scuttling over sand, "will you swear the solemn Oath to me now? Now that you know the *whole* story?" He was sitting again, and staring so hard at me, I thought his gaze would cut me like a knife.

I bit my lip. I was *far* from knowing the *whole* story. And maybe I'd never know it. All who knew the truth of it—but Orybon and Grey—were long dead or perhaps sailed off to the Western Isles, the land of the Ever Fair, from which no fey ever returns. Still, it was probably all I was ever going to get.

"What am I to swear to?" I asked, buying time.

"He does not need to tell you that." Grey's hand was once more on his sword, his mind once more on the prince's wishes.

"I need to think some more about it." I wished I knew what time it was, what hour of the clock, whether it was night or day outside. I wished I could find my spindle and the Cloak. Besides, I was hungry, tired, cranky, and frightened. But I was also worrying a lot, considering options, and needed to be away from the two of them for a while.

"What is there to think about?" Grey asked.

Before I could answer, Prince Orybon said to Grey, though his eyes never left me, "She is a child, Grey, and has been subjected to much this day. Let her sleep. We have the time." His smile was not pleasant. "*All* the time in the world."

Cranky himself, Grey turned on him, for once his hand off the sword hilt. "Now she's a *child* again? Would you have it only *when* you wish, *how* you wish?"

His cousin shrugged.

"*What* you Wished brought us here, you know."

Orybon turned toward Grey slowly, the slowness deliberate to show his disdain. He spoke equally slowly, in a kind of drawl. "I know. Do not task me with it again. *I* was sent here. *You* chose to come."

Grey sighed, an awkward sound, as if he wasn't used to doing so. "I chose because you were to be king, and I was your right hand. Because I'd been brought over as a child from the other court to be both hostage and friend and thought I was a friend and forgot that I was a hostage. But *you* did not." His face looked almost haunted. "You *never* forgot that." He hesitated, and I thought he was about to say something he'd never said before so I listened with care. "*And* because I was loyal. You have to grant me that."

Orybon shrugged again, a casual, elegant gesture, as if there were no bones in his shoulders, only something like river water flowing over an unseen bottom. As if the loyalty of his cousin was expected and needn't be mentioned. And then he mentioned it. "And because you, of all my family, loved me."

Grey didn't contest that, only said, "Your father told you that you would be freed when you truly regretted . . . I thought it would be merely a matter of days. Or a matter of weeks. What does a boy know of time? But of course by then it was too late."

Once again the prince shrugged. "I *am* regretful."

"But not truly. Or we would have been recalled already."

"How is your father to know . . . ?" I asked, forgetting to just listen.

"He'd know . . ." Prince Orybon said, but to Grey as if I hadn't spoken.

That was when I realized they didn't actually have any idea how long they'd been imprisoned, that there'd been three fey generations more while they'd been living and arguing with each other in this cave. I wondered if Fergus and Maeve had married Under the Hill and left when she was pregnant with the first child, or if they'd left right away, before Orybon had time to Curse them further. Or if Orybon and Grey had been immediately transported down here after the first Curse.

I doubted any of the Uncles who'd fallen down a trap to die here had much knowledge of the family tree. Might not have known Banshee's real name. Might never have heard of Fergus. So how could Orybon and Grey know much?

Time, I thought, *in faerie exile must work the way fey time does with humans.* I alone seemed to know that Fergus had been dead for hundreds of years, a long time even for us long-lived fey, but for Orybon, his Cursed brother was still—and improbably—alive.

I would have laughed in their faces then but quickly decided not to, as I'd no idea how they'd take it. Not without *actually* knowing (instead of guessing) if Orybon could Curse me in the cave, or if Grey would really slice off my head.

But this I *did* know: though these two had outlived all those they'd known in the Unseelie Court, they'd nothing to judge that time against except the generations of cave trolls. *How long,* I wondered, suddenly, *do cave trolls live?*

How often do they reproduce? Are they also subject to the delayed time in the bespelled cave?

I tried to read what the two men knew by staring at their faces in the fading light of the hearth, but they were too deep in their old arguments to offer much. And I wasn't about to enlighten them. Everything I knew that they didn't helped my cause. So I faked another yawn that quickly turned into a real one.

After I gave two or three more rather loud yawns, even Prince Orybon noticed and said, "Go to bed, child." He waved his hand toward the direction of the hearth.

There was a high bed I hadn't noticed before by the fire, made up with a coverlet of pink and gold, under a canopy with drapes of the same colors. A young girl's bed. Not that I'd *ever* slept in pink and gold. I knew at once it had to be a glamour because the draperies were too fresh and clean looking. Besides, there was no way the prince would have slept in such a girl's bed. But even knowing, I went over to it, dragging along as if I could barely lift my feet. Suddenly, my right foot struck something that skittered away from me.

I looked around quickly. The prince and Grey were still deep in their old argument, their backs to me, so I knelt down and felt around. My hand closed about the spindle, still hidden by the Cloak. I must have dropped them here when I Shouted poor Gargle into his grave. I didn't know if the spindle and Cloak could help me, but I picked them up anyway, thinking that *anything* I could find of a magick nature had to be of some use. And anyway, once outside again, I would need them both for the christening. *If* I got there in time.

Time. It was all about time. I'd no idea how long I'd already been Under the Hill and whether time would go slower or faster above. But I hadn't burst into a thousand stars yet, so I held the spindle and Cloak close, climbed up onto the pink-and-gold bed, and lay down, planning to eavesdrop on whatever the two fey were saying.

The beglamoured mattress, whatever it was made of, was soft, and the coverlet warm. I settled between the sheets, the spindle and Cloak still clutched in my arms, meaning to stay awake and listen to the prince and Grey. But before I'd heard another whole round of their arguments, I fell into a real sleep, and all my plans were in vain.

At home, morning always dawns pearly, the chorus of birds singing us awake. But in the cave, there was no dawn, no birdsong, and no light when I woke the first time.

When I woke the second time, it was still dark, silent, clammy, and cold. There was a strange smell around the bed, something sharp and unfamiliar. Something dark and maybe dangerous. But not so dangerous that I could keep myself awake. I hugged the spindle to me, wrapped in the Cloak, and slept again.

The third time I woke, I sat up. The glamoured bed was gone, and I found myself in the middle of a high nest of moss on the stone floor. The spindle was still invisible, though the edges of the Cloak were now showing, like old leaves in the moss. In the hearth, a fire was only fitfully sputtering, which made me believe that it, at least, was real. I realized at last that the pong I'd been smelling all along came from there. I turned my back on it, afraid it might be something awful—or someone awful—burning.

But even though I tried to fall asleep again, sleep would not come, and so at last I got out of the bed, though I left the spindle and its cover still in the moss. Stretching, I suddenly wished I'd water and soap for a good washing, and a cleaner dress. I wished I'd a comb to untangle my hair and a brush for my wings, whose feathers were now sadly matted and filthy.

My wings! I touched the right one tentatively. Though it felt modestly better, I still couldn't flex it without pain. There'd be no flying that day. I stifled tears in the corners of my eyes with a grimy fist.

"Awake at last?"

It was Prince Dry Voice—*Orybon,* I reminded myself—which made me wonder if he ever slept at all. Perhaps the nest of moss *was* his own bed, and he'd been forced to sit upright in the chair all night because of his kindness to me.

Kindness? I gave myself a mental shake. *This is the man who has captured me, taken me away from my Family and the Light.* My thoughts turned cold. *Serves him right.* And then I thought, *Maybe I haven't slept all that long, after all.*

"Hungry?"

Of course I was hungry. But I wasn't going to fall into *that* trap. Not yet anyway. Besides, I had other, more pressing needs.

"Begging your advice, kind prince," I began, though neither one of us was fooled by my politeness. "I have to . . . I've got to . . ."

Thank goodness I didn't need to say further. He pointed to a plain white chamber pot and waved me down a dark corridor. He didn't have to point twice.

I had a bladder ready to burst. I knew all about bladders. *Body* is in the *B* section of the library, a book with diagrams that I found fascinating. Especially the differences between men and women. Even though I have brothers, I knew nothing about their bodies, not being into spying like the twins. Father had showed me the body book and told me that except for the wings and the flight muscles, and a vestigial organ or two (he meant stuff inside that was no longer useful and so we fey no longer had any), our bodies and humans' bodies are completely the same. "So it will be good instruction for you."

So—bladder. Full. Needs emptying. But even more important, this would give me time to explore without Prince Orybon suspecting a thing. I nodded at him, and when he turned away—whether annoyed or bored or embarrassed by my asking, I was never to know—I bent down and gathered up the spindle in the Cloak.

With enough of a head start, I figured I might be able to escape even if I couldn't fly.

Oh, foolish wish, foolish hope. In my heart I knew that. But I also knew I'd be more of a fool if I didn't at least try.

So I walked into the dark corridor, trying to look like someone thinking only about her bladder, which wasn't hard, holding tight to the handle of the chamber pot, which was probably only a be-glamoured rock anyway—and whistling.

Once thirty steps into the dark, I put the Cloak over my head and shoulders, the spindle into the chamber pot, and raced along the corridor until the blackness confused me. Squatting down, I took the spindle out of the pot, did my bladder business quickly, and was just standing—holding the pot carefully so as not to slosh it over myself. And suddenly there was a hard hand on my shoulder.

A voice in my ear, Grey's voice, said, "What have we here, little cousin? You are a long way from the fire. Beware of trolls."

Clearly the Cloak had stopped working again.

I was incensed that he should have been spying on me at such a time. Humiliated, too. Even the twins wouldn't have done such a thing! Without wondering how he could see me in the dark—even with the Cloak malfunctioning—and without ever thinking through the consequences, I lifted the pot, flung its contents into his face, and then broke the pot over his head for good measure. It *was* a pot of some kind, and it shattered.

"Maybe you'll decide against spying on a lady next time!" I yelled at him.

He cried out, fell down, and I was away, running blindly down the corridor as fast as I could. I let my left hand trail along the stone wall for guidance, my right hand held out before me, should I run into a stalactite. It seemed a good plan for the moment.

Suddenly remembering I'd left the spindle on the ground, I hesitated, turned halfway back, stubbed my toe against a piece of rock jutting up from the cave floor, and fell down face forward, with just enough time to remember the other cave word I'd learned in the *C* book.

Stalagmite.

• • • • • • • •

•

This time when I awoke, I was back on the mossy bed with a collar around my neck and a leash in the hand of the prince of laughter.

Prince Orybon was convulsed by my misdeeds. His laugh had no mirth in it, no pity. It felt like a saw against the back of my neck where the collar chafed.

"Grey was soaking mad when he hauled you back," he told me the moment my eyes opened and focused. "Soaking wet, too. And his head is *still* ringing. Most enjoyment I've had in . . . in . . ." He stopped laughing and rubbed his nose as if contemplating for the first time how long it might have actually been. "In a long time," he concluded. "You are quite the accident, little lady."

When my eyes finished focusing, I saw he was holding the spindle as if it were some sort of king's scepter or maybe some kind of fey wand. Without thinking, my hand went to my shoulders. The Cloak was still there, but as he could see me, I guessed it wasn't working. Still.

"How many minutes have I . . . have I been out?" I asked. My head was ringing, too.

"Time is unaccountable here and uncounted," he answered.

"I bet."

"How much?"

Without thinking, I said, "An Oath's worth."

"Done," he said. "You tell me how much time has passed since Grey and I were popped into this prison, and I will not force you to take the Oath."

I thought about that. Would his knowing how long he'd actually been in the cave help him and hurt me, or the other way around? Should I let him know that since my Great-grandfather Fergus had married my Great-grandmother Maeve, there had been generations of children, grandchildren, then great-grandchildren? Or should I just keep silent?

In the end, I figured his knowing some of it might soften him up. It just might save me from bursting into a thousand stars. And get me home in time to save the Family.

All in all, it was a long think. Father would have been proud. And the prince seemed in no hurry for my answer. He'd had quite a while to develop a curious patience, something everyone said I needed to learn.

I counted to a slow ten, about as long as *my* patience could last, nodded at Orybon, and took that bet.

"I am Fergus and Maeve's great-granddaughter," I said, as if I were an only child. *Not a lie, Father,* I thought. *Just not all of the truth.*

"Prove it."

"She was called Banshee." I heard him breathe out suddenly, as if someone had punched him in the stomach. "Now, what is it you want me to do?"

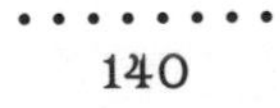

I figured that if I didn't have to take the Oath, I could decide whether or not I could manage the task. And maybe if it was doable, and I did what the prince asked, he would let me go.

"Is Maeve still alive?" he asked. His voice was tight. But controlled. Very controlled.

I didn't answer. Let him make his own guesses.

"Is that pissant Fergus still living?" he roared.

I was silent on that account as well.

"You will take the Oath. NOW!"

"I told you how much time has passed; I won the bet. You said—"

"I lied."

I could almost hear his smile. The last bit of the hearth embers crackled as if scolding me for falling for such an old trick. Still, how could I have known he would do such a thing? No one in the Family ever lied about a bet. No *true* fey would. "But, you said—"

And then someone else laughed, from the shadows.

It was Grey. "Prince of Lies," he said, coming into the firelight. "You will get used to it." He paused and said in a lower voice, "You will have to." Then, in a whisper, his handsome face closed and difficult to read, added, "I have." It was not a plea for sympathy but a heartfelt confession.

"Family love," Prince Orybon said. "Half a mile wide and inches deep."

"You have dug that hole yourself, cousin," responded Grey.

Even with all their bickering, I knew Grey would die for Orybon. When it works right, family loyalty is like that. I didn't dare think about the Family now, or I'd begin to weep aloud. I didn't dare think about how Prince Orybon was my Great-granduncle, though there was nothing great or grand about him at all. I forced myself *not* to think about the spindle in the prince's hand.

I had to think of only one thing—escape.

Well, actually, two.

Escape—and the Oath.

We were a long time in silence after that. Me, because I was afraid to say anything more. Grey because he had nothing left to say. And Prince Orybon because he was laughing at us both, but silently, which somehow made it worse.

At last the prince pulled on the leash hard enough so that I had to stand up in front of him, like a performing bear. Not that I'd ever actually seen a performing bear, except in the *B* section of our library, where the picture is very sad and the bear even sadder.

"What is this thing?" he asked, holding up the spindle.

"A spindle."

"I can see that. What is its use to you here?"

"A present for the princess . . . We were . . . the Family . . . all going to her christening when I fell into your trap."

"What kind of thing is that bit of tat?" He pointed to the Cloak.

I shrugged and closed it over my shoulders. But it was still not working, and I was visible. *And what use is magick,* I thought to myself, *if it only works when* it *wants to, and not when you want it to?*

The prince yanked on the collar again so hard, I was shaken into a coughing fit.

"My prince," Grey said, back in the shadows after his confession, a strange concern in his voice, "you said yourself, she is but a child."

"And wasn't it a moment before that you wanted to take her head?" growled the prince. But he slackened the leash, and I could breathe again.

"It confers long life on a human," I told him. "The thread—"

"Oh, this!" Orybon said, taking a piece of the thread between his hands and casually breaking it into two strands. "I expect your princess will not live long now, so no need to hurry home."

It was possibly the cruelest thing he'd done so far, because it was done in such an offhand way. I didn't know what to say to him, since I'd no idea if the spindle actually worked that way, and I doubted if he knew either. Or cared. I think he did it to make me understand how serious he was.

"Here now is your Oath," Orybon said.

I was suddenly furious, more furious than I'd ever been with anyone. My fists clenched, and I couldn't remember the last time they did that. "An Oath compelled by a lie holds no power," I said, speaking strongly, though I feared that wasn't actually true. I was loud, but not yet Shouting. In fact, in the back of my mind, I wondered if he had any power to compel me. I took some small satisfaction in the possibility that he didn't, though I was careful not to smile.

And perhaps, I thought, *perhaps the broken thread is not so important.*

"Do not be so sure of that, little Shouter," he said, smiling slowly, as if he'd just read my thoughts.

I shuddered, which made him smile even more broadly.

But I was right to shudder. He should have been shuddering, too. The one thing I truly knew about Oaths, besides what happens if you break one, is that the sacredness of them didn't lie in the power of the Oath-maker, but the Oath itself. I'd no idea if a compelled Oath taken in this cave could hold the power to make me burst into a thousand stars if I broke it. Or if perhaps an Oath I was tricked into by a lie might cause the Oath-maker to go the star route. Or if the magick making me sick, the magick that Orybon's father used when he dumped the two men in the cave, changed everything I knew about Oaths, Curses, and magick. The question was—did I want to gamble my life on a guess?

The collar around my neck chafed. My head hurt. My wing hurt. My leg where I was burned hurt. I was angry. I was hungry. I was cold. I missed the Family. I wanted to feel the sun on my face and the wind through trees. I wanted a book in my hand. I even longed to hear my siblings and cousins arguing.

And then I understood: even if I had to murder someone to get back home, I was ready to do so, and this after only one—or maybe two—days in the cave with Orybon and Grey. After all, I'd already killed poor old Gargle without meaning to. The difference between *meaning* and *mistake* was thinner than a spider's strand, and I was already caught in the web.

"Give me the Oath," I said, my voice croaking. "There may be stars out there tonight, but they won't be mine."

"Well said," Grey remarked from the dark, still as invisible as if *he* were covered by the tatty Cloak.

The prince didn't reprove me or Grey this time, but smiled his snake smile. "Hands together."

I said a quick silent prayer to the Magick Lords, in case they could hear me down here, which I was doubting more and more. But it couldn't hurt.

"Now, listen to what I have to say, Pudding Alice, and after, you will swear the Oath."

I nodded. I'd no thoughts other than that nod.

"You will be taken by Grey to Gargle's people, and they will lead you to the Gate."

"There's a *Gate*?" I didn't even notice the mention of Gargle's people. Not then, at any rate. "Why don't you just go through it? Is it magick? Is it dangerous? Is it—"

He yanked the leash again, and I coughed as the collar tightened. "I said *listen*. That does not include talking."

"Majesty . . ." Grey stepped out of the shadow and held up a hand.

Prince Orybon quieted him with a look, but Grey didn't shrivel under that dark glance. Rather he gave the prince back a look of his own. If it came down to a fight between them, at that moment I wouldn't have bet on the outcome.

It didn't matter to me that the two of them were now glaring daggers at one another. After that last yank, I couldn't have spoken if I tried. So I listened. Or at least I tried to look as if I were listening. But I was thinking, too.

"You will say these words at the Gate. Since you have not been banned, have not been Cursed to stay on this side of the wall till your father spares you, you should be all right."

"*Should* be all right?" My voice, or what there was of it, sounded remarkably like a frog's. I hoped the prince would allow those four words without another yank on the leash.

A low mirthless laugh from Grey was followed by a

low, mirthless explanation. "He means you will probably not be dismembered by the McGargle tribe. Or broken into a thousand motes of light by the magick of the Gate. Or—"

Prince Orybon growled. "Now *who* is frightening the child?"

"Now *who* is telling her the truth?" countered Grey.

If they'd been wolves, the hairs on the backs of their necks would have been standing straight up.

"I was already frightened," I croaked. "Of the Oath first and foremost." *And,* I thought miserably, *if the McGargle tribe of trolls tears me to pieces, it's really what I deserve. But I hope they will take my age into account. And the fact that I'd only been trying to escape a creature I thought about to eat me, and—*

"Ah, the Oath," Orybon said. "Because of Grey's interruptions, I had almost forgotten the Oath."

None of us believed that for a second.

"Give me the words . . ." It was almost said as a command, when I should have begged. But I was through with begging.

The prince's voice became very low, slow, melodic, hypnotic. I'd read about hypnosis in the *H* section of the library. I'd read it over about a hundred times and had tried it on my brothers and sisters. Only Dusty fell asleep, waking refreshed, but not under my command.

"You will go to the Gate and recite these words before it," he said.

"Here before you, I—penitent—stand,
Open, Gate, at my command."

"Er . . . what exactly am *I* repenting?"

"She is right." Grey's handsome face was fully lit now by the sputtering hearth. "The Gate won't open if she pretends to be you. And what *does* she have to repent?"

I started to make a list in my head. Leading it was Shouting poor Gargle away. After that came a long list, which included ignoring my sisters, playing tricks on Dusty, not loving my Mother enough, not trying hard enough to be the One . . .

Prince Orybon conceded the point. "Right," he said at last, glaring at me. "You are a fey girl." His hand described a circle in the air. "Make something up."

I stopped creating a repentance list and roared at him. "That's it? THAT'S IT?" My voice had come back with just a touch of hoarseness, and now it rose almost to a Shout. I was no longer holding my hands together but shaking them about. "Here you've frightened me half to death, dragged me around by a collar, kept me from going home, and all you can offer me is *Make Something Up*?"

Grey clapped his hands and began laughing uproariously, which made the prince growl. And below their noise, I thought I heard a scrabbling sound nearby that could have been rats or snakes or the start of a Curse.

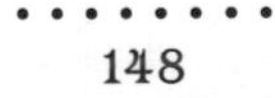

I spun around, looking for that sound, and was brought back by Orybon's voice.

"Once you get the Gate open," he said, "go through and seek out my father. Tell him I give in. I am done with this business. I repent. I regret. I reproach myself. I am sorry for my Curses. My conscience is stricken. I am full of remorse. I am *most* contrite."

"And are you?" I asked, for the more he spoke, the less I believed him. *"Truly?"*

"Of course, *truly*," he said, waving a hand as if dismissing my question as stupid or uninteresting.

"Because, even after taking an Oath, I can't tell your father something I know to be untrue. There's elf in me, and you know they can't lie." My mind was ajumble with thoughts like *I am only half elf, and my fey tricksiness often outweighs the truth telling.* Which of course I didn't say aloud. Instead, I said, "What if your father asks me if you've *truly* repented?" I didn't add, *If he's even still alive to ask me.* Which I doubted.

"You probably should have taken her head when you had the chance." Grey stood with his arms crossed, looking almost bored, but a mischievous smile played on his lips.

"Chances can come again," the prince said. "But done cannot be undone."

I shivered. Even the small, smelly fire couldn't make me warm.

"Got that? Your Oath is that you get the Gate open, find my father, give him my message of repentance." Orybon spoke directly to me, dismissing Grey entirely. "And then you report back here to me, and we will go through the Gate on your promise, my cousin and I."

"And me," I added.

"Of course, you." He said it without conviction. "Now, hands together, swear."

I put my hands together. "I know how to take an Oath." That is, I knew it in theory. Hands together, then the swear. But of course I'd never actually done one. Or seen one done.

"For the gods' sake, child," Orybon said, "just take the Oath already."

"I swear that I will go through the Gate and speak to your father about your repentance and then return to tell you what he says and if it is safe for you to go through the Gate and then go through with you and Grey if it is." I said this with conviction, though I ran out of breath near the end and had to croak the last three words. I'd also crossed my two pinkies together surreptitiously. I didn't actually know for sure if crossed fingers were effective in countering a real Oath, though in games with my brothers and sisters, it always worked.

Prince Orybon didn't seem to notice the crossed fingers, for the minute I swore, he swiftly, but without any kindness, took the collar off my neck. He believed there was no need for it now. It never occurred to him that I—a girl—might choose to burst into a thousand stars rather than do what he commanded.

But Grey *had* noticed. "My prince," he said, taking one step toward Orybon.

"Be quiet."

"She was not—"

"I was, too—"

"Shut up, both of you, and let me think," said the prince.

But it was far too late for thinking and far too late for shutting up. The scrabbling noise was even louder, and before I had a chance for a true Shout, we were surrounded by a huge, hairy family of monstrous cave trolls, their shadows so enormous, they blocked the light and the small bit of warmth from the stinking hearth.

McGargles, I thought, but at least this time I was smart enough to stay silent.

·10·

THE MAGICK GATE

With so many of the huge, hairy males and females surrounding us, the stench was almost unbearable, and so I held my breath. Grey and the prince must have done likewise, because when they spoke, their voices were strained and some of their words were hard to decipher.

"Dake her," Prince Orybon said to the monsters but pointing at me, "do the Gate." Then he turned to Grey. "Add you—go along wid dem."

Grey nodded, and said to me, "Doh rudding off dis dime."

I said nothing, which he took as agreement.

Then one of the McGargles came toward me and slung

me onto his hairy shoulder, and we were off in that rollicking run I remembered from before. It gave me stomach cramps to think of it, of what I'd done to that first McGargle. But I didn't know what to say or how to say it. I kept my apology and guilt inside, though each thought turned into another stomach cramp.

As we loped along, I turned my head and saw Grey with a fiery torch at the middle of the pack of monsters. I wondered how long he'd remain there. Running while not breathing through your nose can't be all that easy.

Even though I was bouncing up and down on the McGargle's shoulder, I watched carefully where they ran. As long as Grey and his torch were close by, I could count the tunnels and how many turns we made. I was up to about five right-hand turns and a single left, but suddenly things got darker. I saw that Grey had fallen behind, because the torch kept getting dimmer and dimmer, and pretty soon there was no light anymore, just slate-gray tunnels, which corkscrewed and turned until I totally lost count of which way was which.

"Oh, Father, oh, Mother," I whispered, a sort of prayer, but didn't get any more than that out because the McGargles had begun singing as they ran, a kind of marching cadence. Or perhaps they'd been singing all along and I'd just been too busy counting turns to listen.

I recognized that kind of cadence because one of the

Uncles had been a general, and before he left, he used to make the boys march around the forest in front of Grandfather Oak, counting off in a singing chant. We girls all took turns glamouring ourselves as one of the boys whenever Alliford or Carnell or the twins wanted to skive off from the marching, which was often. The general never knew the difference. Uncles only saw what they wanted to see. And what *we* wanted them to see. They may have understood about us being the Shouting Fey, but glamour befuddled them. As it was meant to.

Naturally, the monsters' cadence was in the McGargle tongue, and so I didn't know exactly what it meant. But I understood the tone and the pattern. And the count certainly kept them running together.

After a long, twisting run, the cave trolls finally began to slow down and then gave a series of shouts. As we rounded what turned out to be the final turn, before us—partially lit by another hearth fire—loomed an immensely tall Gate, which blocked the tunnel completely. The way the McGargles were acting, it seemed that this area was probably their home base. For one thing, it smelled entirely of McGargle. For another, it was filled with dozens of dark, hairy bodies lying about on the floor. Some were clearly sleeping, some seemed to be cooking over the fire, and some seemed to be playing. On the far side was an enormous body, not hairy at all. Perhaps, I thought, its hairlessness made the others ignore it. Or ostracize it. Or chain it to the rock—though this last was fanciful, as who could have forged any chains?

But all that was beside the point because the smell of the Gate cave was so overwhelmingly monstrous, it all but overpowered me. The McGargles each had a musty, fusty, old mop smell crossed with the nasty stink of a cow's unwashed bottom. A whole tribe of them was . . . well . . . indescribable. Added to that was the strange, sharp, silky pong from the fires. Immediately, I dubbed the place Camp McSmell.

The dark bodies leaped up as we approached, all except the hairless one in the far end of the cave, and I saw over a dozen little McGargles, who greeted us with whoops and howls of joy. These creatures were ugly and coarse, smelly and loud, but they also seemed loving and joyous, not at all like the sour prince or Grey, whose hand was ever on his sword hilt and a mocking smile ever on his lips. There was suddenly a lot of hopping about and hugging, which reminded me of one of our homecomings after the Aunts had arrived back from a holiday flight. Actually, it was *exactly* like that—though clearly the McGargle grown-ups hadn't been gone all that long. Or that far. And of course, the Aunts all smelled of lilac and rosewater.

The McGargle who was carrying me set me down gently

and went over to his family for some hugging and whooping himself, so I wandered over to the Gate to see what it looked like up close.

As I got to about ten feet away, the Gate began to spit red and orange sparks, as if warning me to keep my distance. That close to the Gate, my head began to throb, signaling another headache on its way. But even from there, I could see the Gate was an impressive device made of some kind of metal—though not iron, or I'd already be fainting from the nearness of it.

Possibly silver. I thought. *Or gold.* Though it looked like neither, being a kind of dark gray. Too dark for silver, wrong dark for gold. Whatever metal, it was certainly sturdy and, in its own way, beautiful. Magick, even at its most horrific, always has a great beauty. That's one of its glories, as Father says, one of the ways it seduces.

There were many panels on the Gate, each wrought with a fey design. The light was low because the hairy McGargles blocked much of the illumination that the single large hearth threw. All I really had for light with which to examine the Gate were a couple of torches near the Gate itself, about seven feet away on each side. So I could just about make out a rising phoenix on one panel, a dragon raining fire on another, a unicorn dipping its horn into a pool on a third, a chimera with glaring eyes on a fourth. But I couldn't spot a handle or keyhole anywhere—which didn't matter, as I had no key. Even if I'd had one, I wouldn't have been able to get close enough to use it.

And, of course, I had no spell either.

Make something up, Prince Orybon had said.

But I simply didn't know anything about the Gate, and I'd need information to make up a spell. Or at least I didn't know anything yet. *Maybe,* I thought, *not ever.* That thought scared me most of all.

Without an idea of what to do next, I turned to the McGargles. "Tell me about the Gate," I said slowly and as loudly as I could, hoping they'd understand me better that way. At the same time, I pointed at the Gate, though I expected nothing more than gabble from them.

"The Gate," came a voice, coolly familiar, "is made of adamantine steel covered with a spell of No Egress. It has never been bent, moved, or tarnished under the weight of magick. Or at least never with what little magick the prince and I can muster down here in this misbegotten place."

How Grey had managed to get here so fast was a puzzle. I couldn't imagine that cool presence allowing himself to be carried by a McGargle, and he didn't seem the least out of breath. But he held the torch high, and it didn't waver even a tiny bit. That torch managed to light up the entire

Gate, which was even more impressive now that I could see it whole.

"It is of Seelie design," he added.

"Why not *Unseelie* design?" I asked. "Didn't Prince Orybon's father set it there?"

"Exactly."

I was confused and said so. Or perhaps it was just my throbbing head that was making concentration difficult. "Why would the two courts work together?"

"Because they are not two separate courts at all, but one court long split over small Mutters that became large Matters. It is why child hostages were exchanged, me for Orybon's youngest brother. No heirs or seconds to the throne—we called the seconds 'spares'—could be sent away, you see. Makes us youngest ones useful and dispensable at the same time. Disposable, even, for here am I, disposed and deposed for all eternity."

I said nothing. What he said and how he said it was too sad for comment. And I was afraid if I told him that I pitied him, he'd hate that. But probably my face showed it. Father always said that my face was as easy to read as a map.

As if he didn't notice pity on my face, or chose to ignore it, Grey said, "There were three of them and three of us." He paused. "Six princes in all."

"You left that out of the story."

"It was not important. Or did not seem so at the time.

The Unseelie princes were Orybon, Fergus, and Tam, in that order. And the Seelie princes were Forest, River, and disposable me."

"I knew you were a prince," I said, "from what you'd said before about coming to the court." I didn't add that once I'd gotten past my fear of him, I'd also known he was a prince by his bearing. And his underlying beauty. This close, with the light from the torches, I could see that he was a very handsome man, with none of the snakelike, sinister quality that compromised Prince Orybon's face.

He nodded. "A prince, but neither the heir nor the spare. So I did not really count." He delivered this statement without any bitterness, just spoken plainly, all the while holding the torch higher. Now I could see how the Gate was shaped to the roundness of the tunnel, how it curved at either side and arched into the roof.

"Beautiful, is it not? And deadly to the touch, for Orybon, who was Cursed, *and* the monsters."

"And for you?"

"I do not know," he said.

"You *don't know*?"

"I assume so. The king's Curse was thorough. It covered Orybon and all he held dear. And as you know, I am . . ."

"Loyal." I spoke the word softly. "So you said. However, my Father always maintains that a foolish loyalty serves neither person."

His smile was both sardonic and sad. "Your Father is wise. For an elf."

"You *know* he's an elf?"

He smiled, not that sardonic smile this time but a genuine grin. "Finn's Get, remember? You said elves never lie. But I knew you had elf blood the first time I saw you." His right forefinger described a small arc, then pointed in my direction. "Your ears."

I'd forgotten I'd admitted about Uncle Finn. But I was pleased Grey was also observant. Though I hid my ears under a mop of hair, I resembled Father in that way, not Mother. But I wasn't going to let him see my pleasure. Hands on hips, I growled, "Well, Father *is* wise. *Very* wise. Much wiser than any of the rest of the Family."

"And that includes Uncles and cousins, I suppose." Now Grey was laughing at me.

I didn't care. His hand was nowhere near his sword, because he didn't need to defend his prince from me. Besides, he knew that, without my help—if compelled and forced labor could be called help—he and his prince might remain in the caves forever.

"It *definitely* includes Uncles and cousins," I said. But I smiled to take away the sting of it.

"So, what else would you like to know about the Gate?"

"All of it. Everything you know. Everything the McGargles know. *Everything*."

He set his torch into another holder near the Gate, but not too near, and we began to look at all the parts of the Gate, from the bottom—which we examined while lying on our stomachs—to the top. We even saw the top from the vantage of a McGargle's shoulders, me on the left, Grey on the right. But always a good five to ten feet away from the Gate.

I ignored the headache. This was too important to let myself succumb to sickness. *Just go on,* I told myself. *Grey has, for all these years. And Orybon. Surely you are as good as they. Or better.*

Pointing out some of the panels on the Gate to me, Grey explained their meanings. He told me that the phoenix rises from a fire of its own ashes—which I knew—and that it was a metaphor for what the prince should be trying to do—which I didn't.

He recited a poem about a unicorn that he said his little sister Rose had written. It began

"The pool is still, and deep, and dark.
We make our wishes, and our mark."

He told me a story about the last chimera and how it died.

By the time we were done inspecting the Gate—being careful never to touch any part of it or get within burn distance of the sparks—I was exhausted, and my head felt as if it had been caught in an iron cage. I knew only a little more than I'd started with, though I'd been entertained along the way with tales, poetry, and a song or two by my surprising Seelie cousin, who seemed to have read even more widely than I, though not—I hasten to add—any books from the future. Since he hadn't been able to bring any books along into exile, he'd had to do with the strong memories of books he'd read in the long ago. I was impressed by that.

As for the Gate, this is what I then knew: it was tall, reaching the ceiling, and molded perfectly to each part of the cave wall. There was no space to climb under it or over it without touching it, which was perilous for the princes and probably for me as well. I knew there was no key for the Gate. I knew there was no hammering the Gate down because it was guarded and warded by magick. And I knew this because in the years Grey and Orybon had been exiled, they'd tried everything, using the McGargles to do the touching stuff, which had killed any number of them.

I summed it up and then asked Grey, "Is there more?"

Grey looked at me as if drinking in my essence, which I found unnerving. Finally he said, "I will tell you everything else I know. Whether I think it means anything or not."

"Fair enough," I said, nodding.

"Nothing fair about it," he said, sounding so remarkably like Father, my eyes filled with tears.

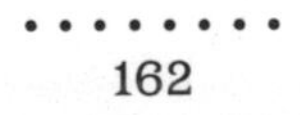

•

We left the Gate and went back to the fire, the cave trolls giving us plenty of room. The hearth gave off a great deal of heat, as well as the strong smell. There were no chairs, but several stalagmites had been smoothed down, and they served as seats, though mighty uncomfortable ones. We sat, our knees almost touching, our backs to the flames.

Grey was telling me a final bit about the McGargles. "The tribe," he said, "want to be able to run through the caves as they had in the great long ago, before this Gate was forced upon them. They want to be able to get out and graze on the berries and wild apples that grow in the meadows all around." His fingers laced together as tight as a withy fence. "It is why they have been willing to sacrifice themselves, not for the prince, but for their tribe." He sighed. "But it has been quite some time since we have explored the Gate. The McGargle losses were just too great. And even Orybon agreed that more hands-on examination was futile in the extreme—it was fast making for an angry peasantry that the two of us could only just manage to control with what glamour we could muster up together." He finished speaking and looked down at his boots.

"I *bet* that annoyed him." The fire on my back was suddenly too hot, and I began to squirm.

"I think it *frightened* him," Grey said thoughtfully,

rubbing a hand through his golden hair. "And that really annoyed him. He is not used to being frightened."

"Just frightening." I didn't say what else I was thinking, that the prince hated not to be the one in control. But I was certain Grey already knew that.

He ignored my remark. It was as if he were the only one allowed to criticize Orybon. "So now you know it all," he said, standing.

I stood, too, wondering, *Do I?* "Let me think about it for a while."

"Think away, little cousin," Grey said, walking far from the fire. I followed him, not trusting myself to be alone with the McGargles, in case I killed another of them.

Grey didn't turn around, but he knew I was right behind him, for he kept on talking. "I, myself, have given up thinking about the Gate anymore. If Orybon would only truly repent—not that stupid recitation of 'give in, regret, reproach, sorrow, stricken, remorse, and contrite,' which he has honed over the years—we could be free. A *true* repentance is what is needed, for then the Gate would simply fall down. But I have no control over him, as you may have noticed."

I ignored that, not wanting to give away what I did and didn't notice or understand. "I don't want to remain here forever," I said.

"Neither do I," Grey answered. "But wanting and getting are hard neighbors and bitter friends."

"Maybe," I said, "maybe now I know enough to try a spell and get through the Gate."

He turned and stared at me. "Are you certain?"

I bit my lip. I had to be honest with him, because as much as he needed my help, I needed his. "No, not absolutely certain. But I have to start somewhere. And as you noted, time is on your side. Though . . ." I sighed, thinking about the christening and the breaking of the Oath of Bidding. "Though it may not be on mine."

"The spell is supposed to be about regret, and there is none on Orybon's part. He is like a child caught stealing sweets from the kitchen. The regret is only that he is caught, he has none for the deed. So there is your dilemma. I would not have you sacrificed on Orybon's honor or lack of it."

He had been totally honest about this, and so I had to give him back as much truth. His courage called out mine. "If I fail at this first hurdle, I don't think I'll burst into a thousand stars," I said. "I think the magick will know I'm trying. The first spell will have to be about *my* regret, not the prince's."

"Ah."

"And yours."

He smiled. "Go on, then. I will stay close by while you try."

So we walked back to the Gate, and once there, I closed my eyes. I began to see the spell as if it had been written out in front of me. Grey was right, it had to have regret built in, and sorrow, and something about the passage of years. It had to be well rhymed and brutally honest. I ran through it a second and a third time. It seemed pretty tight, and honest and true.

I was ready.

I went toward the Gate until it started spitting its orange bits of flame at me. Then I stopped, raised my arms, and began the spell.

Great-great-grandfather, spell for spell,
There's something that I have to tell:
Regret, remorse, imprint these walls.
And every little fey who falls
By trap, by accident, design,
Is caught in magick so malign,
That she is in true danger grave
Unless she can escape this cave.
So help me now confound this fate
By opening the magick Gate.

And then I added, in case that wasn't strong enough, our regular Shouting Fey Spell of Opening, which was related to the trunk spell.

Come thou, door and gate,
Open up, do not be late,
All out!

I raised my voice on the last two words, but didn't Shout. I was saving the Shout for later, should it be needed.

The Gate groaned, and clattered a bit, and for a moment, I thought it might open.

But then, as if it had given us all it could, it went silent again.

"Well," Grey said, "I suppose we shouldn't have expected it to be that easy."

My disappointment must have showed on my face, for he added, "It was a good spell, though, Pudding. Still, you are not yet the magick maker that my uncle is."

Or was, I thought. For if Orybon's father, who made the original spell for the Gate, was as dead as I believed him to be, I should never have mentioned him at all. But it was too late to explain this to Grey, for already my headache had announced itself again. This time, it felt as if an iron blade had pierced my skull. Surely, it would be another day before I'd be able to do anything other than stay in bed whimpering.

If there was a bed to stay in.

·11·

DREAM

Seeing I was about to fall over, Grey picked me up and carried me from the Gate. We were no longer enemies, but still far from friends, even bitter ones. More like comrades thrown together in a war.

He found me a bed of moss undisguised by glamour.

I thought, *As long as it is soft.*

One of the little McGargles came over and crawled in beside me, like some kind of tame baby bear. For a moment, I thought about kicking it away, afraid the smell would make me sicker. It turned out little trolls are not very hairy or smelly at all, sort of a mix between a rabbit smell and a red squirrel. I stroked its head, and it made a kind of *rumbly-bumbly* noise that seemed to resonate through its bones and into mine, soothing my poor head a bit. We snuggled together and Grey shrugged out of his jacket and put it on top of the two of us.

How much nicer the smelly McGargles seemed than Orybon, who'd ruled over them for so many years. They were simple, uncomplicated, joyous. If I could open the Gate and only let the tribe range free again, I'd be doing them a huge favor. And maybe, just maybe, that would make amends for killing one of them. If the prince and Grey got out of the cave as well, I wouldn't complain. It would save me from bursting into a thousand stars.

But how to bring the Gate down without killing us all?

How to convince my Great-great-grandfather—if he was still alive—to take back his not-quite-regretful son and heir?

Or if Great-great-grandfather was dead and gone, and the rest of the Under the Hill folk with him, could I persuade the Aunts to take in the two unpredictable Seelie/ Unseelie men?

And how long was it going to take?

I'd more questions than answers. And it all began with getting past that Gate.

Giving the little McGargle a soft pat on the head, and wrinkling my nose just a bit, I closed my eyes.

•

I fell headlong into a dream. In it, I was a hostage in a high stone castle looking deep into a hearth fire that shed no warmth and little light. In the center of the hall, a chimera fought with a knight in gray armor for the kingdom's crown. I jumped up, raced between them. Snatching the crown from the throne, I threw it at the castle door, where it exploded in a burst of stars.

I woke before I could see if the dream door was completely down. The baby McGargle was fast asleep next to me in the moss, thumb in its mouth. I'd no idea how long I'd slept, but my head seemed reasonably clear. That, if nothing else, was a great start for the escape.

Careful not to unsettle the little troll, I crawled out of the moss bed, all the while thinking, *Dreams can be read like a book.* How often Father had told me that. Everything in a dream has its counterpart in life, though one must puzzle it out. I'd found out more about dream reading in the *D* section of the library, and understood then it was not just a fancy of Father's but something that people far in the future know for a fact.

So I started thinking about all the different things in my dream, hoping they might help me figure out how to bring down the Gate.

The knight in armor was surely Grey, I thought. *So, then the deadly chimera had to be the prince.*

I scratched at my head. Really—it was past time for a

hair wash. And then I told myself, *After*—meaning *after* the Gate came down.

And the castle door in the dream? The Gate, of course.

Oh, I thought, *I'm* really *understanding this dream-reading stuff!*

I almost danced with delight.

But what about the hearth fire? The crown? The throne? I bit my lower lip and thought some more. *Was the hearth fire anger, passion, hot blood? Were the crown and throne supposed to be read as real, the kingship of the Unseelie Court? Or was one of them supposed to be the Oath?*

I went around and around thinking about it until my head began to ache all over again from doing that amount of thinking. And from the magick that continuously leaked from the Gate.

Perhaps, I thought, *perhaps it's something simpler. Perhaps the fire is simply . . . fire.*

"Fire." I said it aloud. "Hearth fire."

I went over to the nearest hearth, stared down into the flickering flames, looking at the place the hot embers . . . *should* have been.

Suddenly, I realized that not only were there no embers . . . there were no logs either. None. Instead the fire was set in a large natural cauldron filled with an odd dark lake of burning liquid. It reminded me of something—and then I had it—

Grey's sister's poem:

"The pool is still, and deep, and dark,
We make our wishes, and our mark."

I leaned over, gazing deeper into the fire before I understood. There was plenty of heat. But the smell . . . was not at all like wood smoke. It was that odd pong.

So, I thought, *for centuries these hearth fires had been kept burning by the McGargle tribe for warmth. They—and presumably the two fey men at their own hearth—have cooked in the fire's small flames and eaten by its small light.*

I mumbled aloud, trying to reason the fire thing out, "The prince's great fire may be partially glamoured, but surely not here where the McGargles camp. There'd be no reason for Orybon to waste his glamour on these creatures when they are off alone. I mean, they lived in the caves long before he was ever sent here as punishment, so they must have had these fires before he ever came."

Think, Gorse, think!

So, I thought, *not glamoured fire, and not glamoured food. At least* something *here is real.*

My growling stomach asked me the next questions. *Where has the fire come from, then? And where the food?*

Suddenly I realized that the dream hadn't been about

bringing down the Gate at all. It was simply helping me solve a puzzle that my eyes had observed but my brain hadn't begun to figure out. Would it help me eventually with the greater puzzle of the Gate? I didn't know that . . . yet. But at least I knew I could eat something without fear of being bewitched.

"At court, we call that fire stuff *oyl.*" Grey was at my side. I wondered if he'd heard what I'd just said, then realized it hardly mattered.

"*Oyl*?" It wasn't a word I'd ever heard, and even if it was mentioned in the library, I wasn't close to the *O*'s yet.

"*O, Y, L.*" He spelled it out. "It is a liquid that burns forever, or so it seems. The cave walls weep with it. Do you not have that where you live?"

I looked at him wryly. "I don't live in a cave, prince, but up above. In the woods and meadows and . . ."

He smiled at my calling him a prince, then shook his head. "I assumed you Shouters lived in a cave *beside* the woods."

"In a belvedere, actually."

He said *belvedere* back at me the way I'd said *oyl* to him, a moment before.

"*B, E, L, V, E, D, E, R, E,*" I said, mimicking his preciseness. "It's a kind of house with . . ." I tried to describe its domed roof and winding stairs with my hands, and failed.

"And you *built* these?" He was clearly astonished.

"I think the royals whose Bidding we do built them long ago. Not as houses, actually, but as . . . well, as pretty displays hidden in their vast gardens."

He folded his arms and looked at me searchingly. "You do someone else's Bidding, someone who is *not* a fey?"

I nodded, suddenly reluctant to admit it.

"What kind of princess *are* you?"

This time I was the one who laughed. "I never said I was a princess."

He thought for a minute, then stared at me, his face unreadable. "Ah, I see that now. *You* never said you were a princess."

I didn't enlighten him. If Fergus could have been king, I suppose I *was* a princess.

"So that was just Orybon's fancy," Grey said. "He cannot believe, even down here, that someone with power and backbone can possibly be less than his equal in rank. Except for me. He knows quite well where I dangle on the chain." He stood quietly for a bit more, now staring down at the cave floor, strange looks passing across his face like an army on the move. Suddenly, he bit his lip, almost like a boy, before saying at last, "Perhaps you are worse off up there in your belvedere than the prince and I are down here in our cave. At least our fate is in our own hands."

"Your fate is in *his* hands," I pointed out.

"Yes, it is, but I put it there, more shame to me." His voice no longer seemed either sarcastic or angry but was, in fact, rather sad.

For the first time, I actually liked Grey. Or at least for the first time, I didn't actually hate him. At that moment, I thought those things were the same.

"You . . . you aren't here because of loyalty or love," I said, suddenly recognizing what had been before me all this time. "You swore an *Oath*!"

He looked at his feet. "I was thirteen. And far from home."

"And *he* was how old?"

"Twenty-five. A man."

"So *he*, at least, knew what he was doing."

"Alice Pudding, or whatever your name is," Grey said, looking so deeply at me, I thought he could see into my heart, "you are quite a one."

I mistook him. "No. I am not the One."

Suddenly bemused, he looked his old sardonic self. "*The* One?"

"The One to save you and the Unseelie prince." I didn't mention what that meant to the Aunts and Mother, and I didn't mention saving myself as well or bursting into a thousand stars. I didn't have to.

His face suddenly reminded me of Father's when he'd told me about how we were tied forever to the land.

"If you will not do," Grey said, his voice soft, "no one will."

"Probably that," I whispered.

If he heard, he said nothing in response.

One of the McGargles—impossible for me to tell them apart with all that hair—came over and made sounds rather like a cow in labor. He . . . she . . . held out a hairy hand. There was something meaty in it. I didn't like the look of the meat—it was all mushed and had little bits of bone sticking out—but at least it smelled well cooked. As I'd read somewhere, but couldn't recall where, hunger is a great seasoner.

"She is offering you dinner," Grey said. "Better take it. You have not eaten since falling down here."

I took the messy thing, but not before making a face at it.

"She had better offer *me* some, too." He mooed back at her, and the monster scampered off, presumably to find more of the meat.

"It's real, isn't it?" I asked, and was pleased when he nodded.

"Real as I am. Not glamoured by Prince-All-About-Me."

"Prince-All-About-Me?" I giggled.

"Well, he is not all about *you*," Grey said. "Or," he added, jamming a thumb toward his chest, "not all about the fate of his Oath-man, either."

For a moment, I wondered if Grey was just trying to win me over, then decided to take what he said as simple, straightforward, honest. I pinched a bit of the meat with two fingers, took out the largest pieces of bone, and put half of the meat into my mouth. It was warm and sweet and delicious.

"Fish?" I asked.

"Underground streams," he said. "It is either that or bats. A seemingly endless supply of both. Oh—and mushrooms."

I wrinkled my nose. I hated mushrooms, dingy gray things. And the bats didn't sound at all appealing.

"You can get used to anything," Grey said.

"I guess you'd have to, if you're here a long time."

"Occasionally a cow or rabbit falls into one of our traps. And . . . other things."

I thought about the Uncles going back and forth on the Wooing Path. He couldn't mean that, could he? Surely the prince and Grey hadn't eaten any of . . . no! It didn't bear thinking about. I shook my head.

As if he guessed what I was thinking, he shook his head in return. "We are not cannibals here. But a man falling down one of those traps without wings to slow his fall rarely lives very long. It is why we always hoped for a fey." He said it matter-of-factly, as a soldier would count the cost of a battle.

I chose to believe him. I chose not to ask how many

human men had actually fallen down one of the traps and died. Or what they looked like. Or if any had taken an Oath. Though Oaths don't mean the same to humans as they do to fey. All I knew was that some had talked about the Shouting Fey. For now, that was enough.

"So once you have eaten, and until the McGargle gets back with something for me as well, let us think about the Gate."

The Gate. I'd almost forgotten about it.

I wanted to savor the food, mostly so I didn't have to think Gate thoughts right away. But hunger got the better of me, and I gobbled up the rest of the fish and was sucking what bits remained on my fingers when the monster returned with something for Grey.

He ate slowly, smacking his lips over the meat and the—ugh—mushrooms, a most unprincely sound. Then he laughed at my grim face.

"I taught the creatures how to cook, and they taught me how to show I like it. Besides taking Oaths—and heads"—he winked at me—"cooking is my one great trick. When I was first at Orybon's court, I was so homesick and lonely, I spent a lot of time in the kitchen, where no one made fun of me. So I talked to cooks and told stories to the pot boys, and things . . . just rubbed off on me."

It was such a homely confession, I had to smile at him, which encouraged more admissions.

He said, “When we found ourselves here—Orybon and I—the tribe had only eaten their meat raw, even though they were practically drowning in oyl. We introduced them to cooked food. They had already learned to make fire on their own. They are not stupid, you know, just a bit . . .”

“Smelly?”

He laughed. “*Very* smelly. It’s the hair, mostly. They never wash it, and it manages to keep hold of everything they rub up against, bat droppings, oyl, mushrooms, fish bones, bits of stone. By the time they are grown, they are walking midden piles. And yet”—he took a deep breath—“and yet, they have become wonderful cooks, and each generation has taught the next. We never have a banquet now without them doing the cooking.”

“Did you teach them to dance, too?” For now I knew where the court had come from: glamoured McGargles!

“Orybon did, for entertainment. But they never look as if they are having much fun,” he said, “only counting out the steps of the pavane in Gargle-talk.”

“I noticed.”

“And figured it out right away, I am sure.”

I smiled and let him think so. Then I remembered the tribe’s cadence count, but didn’t ask if he’d taught them that or if it had been one of the Uncles.

“If we ever get out of here,” he said with a sigh, “I want

to learn how to get things for the tribe that will make their lives easier."

"What kinds of things?" I asked.

"Carts, kitchen implements, fishing poles, that sort of thing." Grey finished his bat-and-mushroom meal and then, torch in hand, led me to the underground river, where we washed the meal down with several handfuls of clear, clean, cold water.

"Have you ever tried to follow the river out?" I asked as we walked back to the McGargle hearth.

"Three times. But the water is much too frigid, and the passage where it runs through the stone too narrow. I thought I would never get warm again after the second try. But of course, I did."

I didn't ask him if the prince had gone into the river with him. I didn't have to.

"Now," he said, "we heat water for baths, though we have never been able to convince the tribe to try one. I think they fear water too much. With that much hair, they'd stay wet for far too long."

Suddenly there was a huge rush of sound, like a wild wind. It filled the chamber and whooshed through the corridors. With it came a strange, high keening.

"What's that?" I started to tremble, thinking of more monsters. Angry ones. Not like the McGargles.

He laughed. "Night chorus," he said. "Bats on the move. They go out all at once, like a great black wind."

"Oh," I said, "I don't speak Bat."

He looked at me strangely, then laughed, stopping only when he saw I was serious. "What do you speak?"

Just as serious, I replied, "Hawk, Jay, Crow." Suddenly, I realized what he'd said. "Going out where?"

"Out to where you and yours live."

"But why haven't I heard them down here before? That's a pretty loud noise."

"You were sleeping, child. It seemed an unkindness to wake you for that. I thought there would be plenty of . . ." He hesitated, then plunged on. "Plenty of time for you to see them."

"You don't really believe I'll get the Gate open." I said it flatly, without blame, without expecting an answer.

He had the grace to look down at his feet. Orybon would just have laughed.

"No," he said at last, "I do not believe a thirteen-year-old can manage that. After all, Orybon and I are grown men. In fact, I suspect that we are much older than we look. I can tell the McGargles apart and know how many generations we have been with them. Orybon does not even bother to try. So I have some idea of how long a time we have been down here, trying to figure out an escape plan. All without success."

Longer than you imagine, I thought. "How do the bats get out?"

"Through small apertures in the ceiling. And come back in again at dawn the same way. They roost hanging upside down from the cave roof." He pointed where the cave arched high over us, so high I couldn't actually see the ceiling. "That is what gave us the idea for faerie traps."

I'd read all about bats in one of the books on the *B* shelf. About their ability to navigate by echoes. About their bat droppings, called guano. About diseases they carried. But I didn't mention any of that to him.

"Well, then, maybe I'll have time to learn their language," I said.

"Will you teach me?"

"If you wish. After all, you learned McGargle, so I suspect you'll be able to pick up Bat."

"Easier to get close to a cave troll than a bat and point out things."

I laughed. My, that felt good!

Suddenly I spotted two tiny pinpoints of light in the ceiling above. "Look!"

"Stars," he said.

Never had I seen anything so glorious as those two stars shining through the small opening in the cave ceiling, even better than magicks. Soon, the two stars turned into ten, crowded into the small space. I shivered, thinking that I might soon become such tiny points of light.

I looked back at Grey. *Prince Grey,* I reminded myself. "Have you tried—"

"Before you ask, we do not have the resources to build a ladder that high. We never got any farther than a rickety thing twice my height, and by then we had used up all the wood we could find. I expect that even if we actually had gotten all the way up, the aperture would have been too small for any of us to get through." He looked at me, head cocked. "Even you."

I nodded. It seemed a likely guess.

"How is your right wing?" he asked.

"How did you know?"

"I watched you sleeping, and every time you turned on it, you whimpered and turned back. Did you land on the wing when you fell through the trap?"

I nodded.

"Well, when it heals, perhaps you could fly up and see if there is any room to wiggle through. You could possibly escape through that hole, since it's not a magick trap, but as for the rest of us . . . even if we could get up that high, any leap down could prove disastrous. As you may recall, Orybon and I were Cursed wingless by his father, just as a precaution." He turned to show me his back.

And of course, now that he was in just his shirt, the jacket still over the sleeping McGargle child, I could see there was no outline of wings. It made his winglessness real to me in a way it hadn't been before.

"I wasn't . . . wasn't sure Prince Orybon was telling the truth."

"You are right to be cautious with the prince," Grey said carefully, turning around again. "He tells a lie and convinces even himself that it is true."

"Does that . . . hurt?" I asked, pointing to his back.

"Sometimes it aches, as if a pair of phantom wings are there."

"I'm so sorry," I began, and could think of nothing else to say, but my eyes got cloudy.

"Orybon learned his cruelty at his father's knee," Grey said quietly. "But this exile is not all a bad thing. His brother Fergus will have made a much better king. He's noble and kind and—"

"But still Unseelie." As I said it, I trembled when I realized that Grey didn't know about the exile. So he and the prince must have been sent immediately to the cave after the Curse by Orybon's furious father.

He shrugged. "Sometimes a name is given because of the nature of a people. Sometimes they grow into it."

It took me a moment to remember that he was talking about the Unseelie folk, so absorbed had I been with my latest realization. But he sounded so much like Father, the tears I'd almost shed at his winglessness now prickled in my eyes. So I shook my head to clear it and said carefully, "The opening up there where the bats go out *might* be on the ground."

"It might. But there's no use guessing. We have no more wood to build a ladder. Believe me, we have scoured every inch of these caves, all the winding corridors and smaller caverns. Many times over the long years we have gone on expeditions to find more wood, as have members of the tribe."

And since they'd had many, many years to do it, I didn't doubt him. But I didn't mention that, when my wing healed, I could possibly fly them each up to inspect the ceiling. I was reacting to his trust in me, but as soon as I had that thought, I had a counter-realization. There was no way I could carry either one of those big men up that high without possibly killing both of us.

By this time, we'd walked back to the Gate. It loomed before us. Glowered at us. All but called us names.

Suddenly, I knew what I had to do, knew what the only thing I *could* do was. I wondered that it had taken me so long to see that. It was the only thing different from anything they'd already tried. And it had been in my dream as well.

Turning to Grey, I said, "Get all the McGargles back as far as possible, way back in the corridors. The littlest ones the farthest away. Put solid rock and many corridors between them and me."

"What are you going—" he began, but he already knew.

"I'm going to Shout the Gate down, of course," I said. "It's the only sensible thing to do."

"After the spell and what it did to you, the *sensible* thing for you would be to rest up more."

"Don't tell me what I can and can't do!" I said, my voice rising.

"Madam, I would never *tell* a Shouter female what to do," he answered calmly, though there was a hint of laughter behind his eyes. "The men who fell down the magick traps were quite in agreement on that point, however they differed on your history. But I might *suggest*!"

"Right. Then let *me* suggest that you get those McGargles away, and I will worry about my headaches and wing aches, *Prince* Grey." I turned and walked toward the Gate.

I should have realized that sense and magick needed to go together. I should have been more cautious. But I was only thirteen.

And, like Grey had been when he swore his Oath to the prince, I was equally far from home.

·12·

THE SHOUT

Immediately, as if he'd been ordered by a general or a king, Grey began explaining, cajoling, and then actually pushing the McGargles away from the Gate. Slowly but with great energy, he rounded the big creatures up, shepherding them down the long corridor, including the hairless one who seemed to be shivering once away from the fire.

"McGargles halloooo!" Grey shouted, rather like a cowherd or a pirate rounding up a group for a long trek.

I watched them disappear around a turn and knew he was getting them as far from the Gate as possible. Farther, I hoped. I didn't want to kill anyone ever again.

Since I'd no idea how long to wait for them to get settled,

I simply paced in front of the Gate. All the while, the magick embedded in the Gate made my headache start up again. I wondered if by trying out the spell, I'd made a connection with that magick and given it the ability to sneak into my head. I'd ask Father when I got home.

If I get home. That thought made my head throb again.

The only thing to do was ignore it and make certain everything I had to do was firmly in mind. This one Shout might be the only chance I'd have before the Gate's magick shut me down completely, so I had to make it count.

Unlike the Shout I'd pushed out when enclosed in Gargle's arms, this one was going to have to be well thought through. That would take some time, but time was the one thing I'd plenty of. So, I rehearsed the steps to come: the deep breath drawn in, the open mouth, the Sweetened Spot from which the fuller breath for the Shout would come. And then the actual rush of air out into the Shout, while simultaneously I'd make the Wish.

I thought about the Three *T*'s: *timbre, temper, tension.*

And then I thought about how to frame the Wish.

It couldn't just be a Wish for the Gate to fall down. I understood that. The falling Gate had to be told to fall either forward or back. It had to be disarmed in a way that we could cross over it. Since neither Grey nor Orybon could fly over it and I—for the while—was equally incapacitated, this was an important point.

I wondered briefly if I should discuss everything with Grey first. I was beginning to rely on his sensibleness the way I did on Father's. But he was already hiding well behind the stone walls with the trolls. Yet I really, *really* needed to talk it through with someone who knew more about magick than I did.

But who?

Turning back to the Gate, I thought, *Why the hurry? I've already missed the christening by days. I can only hope that since I'm still alive and not in a thousand starry pieces, the Family is the same. Though why I should think that . . .*

Still, nothing needs to be done this moment. Or today. Or even tomorrow. Except . . . except I want to be home safe. With Father and Mother and the Family. And if—as I partially accepted—I were already too late for that, then . . .

Pictures of starbursts danced before me. Or else my mind was melting.

An enormous shadow moved into the cavern toward me.

I waved my hands at it. "All McGargles out of here. Now—"

"I am hardly a monster," came Orybon's dry voice.

"You most of all, prince."

How could he be *so* stupid? And why was his shadow *so* wide?

And then I saw he'd someone with him. A small troll, perhaps, who limped along by the prince's side.

“Hi, Goosey,” called out the shadow. “I’ve found you.”

“Not Pudding Alice after all?” said Orybon, though he’d never been fooled.

“Dusty,” I whispered, but under my breath, not willing to give the Prince of Lies more than one name at a time, even if it was only Dusty’s pet name for me. Though I was happy to see Dusty, deliriously so, actually, still I was devastated he was here, so close to the monstrous prince. It changed—well—everything.

Aloud, I said in as calm a voice as I could manage, “How, by the gods, did you get here?”

“Fetch, found, flew, fell,” Dusty said.

“Fetched what?”

“Father sent me to fetch you. The king wouldn’t allow us to give any gifts without all of us there after Father explained about you being so sick. He gave us three more days to come back, laughed and called it ‘a damned magick number for you magick makers.’ And Father didn’t want to chance the king changing his mind so that we all burst into—”

“A thousand stars . . . yes, I know.” Those same stars were once again bursting inside my brain.

Dusty ignored me, so breathless in his telling, his hands flailed about. “So Father sent us all off in different directions to find you, since when we’d gotten home, you weren’t there. I chose to fly over the Wooing Path because it's the quickest way between home and castle, and I figured you might go that way in a hurry. I was looking down and saw something sparkling below. I hesitated for a moment. Flying the path isn't forbidden, *walking* it is."

"Mr. Magpie," I whispered.

Dusty continued as if I hadn't spoken. "I thought about the Forbidding, but if that sparkle was a clue to your whereabouts, I had to take the chance. And when I landed," he said, "there was something lying in the grass by a tree: a patch of spiderwebs."

I touched the ripped place in Solange's dress.

"And I found your hair ribbon, too. When I spun around to find you, I fell down some sort of a trap hole. No wonder we're not supposed to go on foot along the Wooing Path. Flew at the last, so I landed easily, except I think I may have hurt my ankle. Your accident thing may be catching, like an ague. And once down and here—wherever here is—I bumped into Sir What's His Name here. Hard hands."

"Harder heart . . . Why didn't you just fly back up and alert the others?"

"I didn't know you were actually here."

"Well, fly away now." I tried to wave him away with my hands. "I don't need you."

"Do too!"

"Do not!" Why couldn't he see that if he left, he could fetch the others? And then I remembered—he could fall *into* the trap but not fly out. Well, maybe he could squeeze through the bat hole.

"Children, children," said Orybon, but he was smiling as he spoke. "Much as I am finding this family reunion infinitely amusing—"

"Stay out of this," I said. And then realized I may have just stepped entirely over the line. What would he do to me? What would he do to *Dusty*?

To my astonishment, he laughed. "What a talkative family you are. Are there more of you at home?"

"Hundreds," I said quickly, holding up a hand so Dusty would just shut up.

"Well, so here is part of the hundreds to help you figure out—"

"Leave him with me," I said, even though interrupting the prince a second time might really be pushing it. But still, he had to be nice to me until . . . well, until he realized I couldn't do what he wanted. "We'll make something happen together."

"A *double* Shout," said Orybon, clapping his hands. Then he laughed again. "I guessed you were going to do one when I saw all the McGargles gathered down the path."

"You knew from the beginning that I'd have to do it." *Even before I knew,* I thought.

"A good warrior understands his weapons."

And of course that was all I was to him, a weapon. And now Dusty was another. The third, Grey, was no longer particularly useful, except to keep the peasants quiet.

"And a good leader knows when to retreat so that the weapon can be used," I told him. I remembered the General telling us that.

Orybon gave me a nod, left Dusty, and moved away.

I called after him, "I'm not giving a Shout until I have that spindle back. In good order."

He turned and held it up. "I thought you might want it!"

I put my hand out for it.

"When the Gate is down, you will get it."

"Your Oath on that, prince."

He laughed. "Why, of course," he said. But his hands were never together, so I didn't know if he meant it or not. Or if that counted as an Oath. But Dusty had heard. And Grey, too. I saw his shadow, with his hand on his sword. Again. But this time it might not have been for me.

And then the two of them were gone, hiding behind the walls of stone with the hairy creatures, leaving Dusty and me alone.

"What's this all about, Gorse?" Dusty whispered when Prince Orybon was truly gone.

I showed him the Gate and then told him everything

I knew about it. I told him what I'd guessed. I told him what I feared. And finally I said, "But which way should I Wish the Gate to fall?"

"Either way, the trolls we passed getting here will have to leap over it in case it's still dangerous," he said.

"Do you mean the troll monsters or the fey monsters?" I asked.

"There's more than one of him?"

"Another, actually, though he's not really a monster but a fey captive as much as we are."

"We, of course, can fly," Dusty said.

"Well, I can't. Not yet." I shrugged. "Hurt it when I fell."

"Poor Goosey," he said, "but I am not surprised."

"The fey men can't fly either. They were Cursed into winglessness when they were imprisoned here."

"Well, I will carry you in my arms, the way I did when you were still too little to fly," he said, poking his finger at me. "You don't look like they've been overfeeding you! Let me see that wing."

I took off the useless Cloak and tied it carefully around my waist. Then I offered my back to Dusty, who explored the wing with his fingers.

I winced at his touch.

"Not broken."

"I know that."

"Probably strained."

"Figured that out, too."

He put his hands up as a gesture that he was giving up any argument. "Then my offer still stands. We get that Gate down, and I will carry you across. Or if we don't get the Gate down, then we fly out of here through the same hole we fell through."

"Can't."

He looked puzzled.

"Magick traps only work one way."

"Did old Prince Hard Hands tell you that?"

I nodded.

"Well, maybe he's wrong. Or lying."

"Or maybe we can fly up there," I said, pointing to the bats' bolt hole.

"Why didn't you show me that first?"

I shrugged. "There's still the small matter of my . . . my Oath."

"Did you have your fingers crossed?"

"Of course. But if you think I trust my life to a children's game—"

He gave me a hug. "Right!" he whispered in my ear. "Let's do that Shout." He stepped back. "You smell, Gorse."

"You try sleeping in a mossy bed next to a baby troll."

He laughed, but held his nose with his fingers just to make the point.

"So, here's what we'll do," I said. "I'll make up the Wish part, and you join me on the count of three for the Shout. Having two of us should be much better than just the one."

He nodded. "Always is." For a moment, he cocked his head to one side and looked at me oddly. "You're not fourteen yet."

"I know."

"And untrained."

"I know."

He grabbed my hands. "You know I'm pretty good on stone walls." Then grinning, he took it back. "Actually, the only stone walls I've ever brought down were the ones quarried and set up by a farmer in his fields. Lots of sparkly stuff in the stones."

"Poor farmer," I said.

"Not really. There was a fortune in gold coins under the wall. He's got a mansion now and a daughter marrying a duke."

"Did you know?"

"Of course I knew. I took out the shiniest and left the rest."

I smiled. Of course he did. But we still had the Gate to worry about. "All right, then we're ready." I spoke more positively than I felt. I'd *no* idea what could happen with two of us Shouting together. It could be a total waste of magick. Or the entire cave could collapse on our heads.

He took my hand. "I'm ready when you are, sister."

I looked steadily at him, the one brother I could always count on. "I'll start on *And.* Then on *One,* we'll do the intake of breath, on *Two,* the open mouth, and then on *Three . . .*"

"The push out of breath."

"The Shout."

He nodded, his normally smiling face suddenly serious as if he'd just realized how fraught with danger all this was.

"Come on," I said. "We'll get as close to the Gate as we dare."

We began to move forward slowly, until the Gate started to spark at us, the orange and red flicking out like dragon tongues. I knew we could have gotten a foot closer on our bottoms, but then we wouldn't have been in any position to run away if things went awry.

And whenever *I* was involved with something, things *always* went awry!

"I'll Wish that the Gate falls away from us," I whispered.

"Good idea. Don't want to be crushed." He laughed out loud, almost as if this were just a lark with the Family boys, though the laugh was strained.

I wanted to smile back, but this wasn't a faerie tale, and

I wasn't certain we were going to get a happy ending. At best, no one would be hurt. Or hurt too badly. At best, we all got out, even Prince Orybon. *Well,* I thought, *that might not actually be for the best!* My lips pulled into a thin line. *At worst . . .*

I forced myself to stop thinking that way. Bad thoughts warp magick.

"I'm not even sure if our magick works here," I said, neglecting once again to mention Gargle and how he disappeared after my first—my only—Real Shout. "I tried a spell on the Gate before you got here, maybe a few hours ago."

"Maybe?"

I shrugged. "Time is funny here."

"What happened?" he asked.

"Not much." I added quickly, "It was a good spell. Great-aunt Gilda would have loved the rhymes."

"I'm sure it was," Dusty said. "But with two of us, any Shout and any spell will be that much better." Always positive, but I could tell he was having second thoughts. Maybe even third thoughts.

As was I.

Still, he held out a hand.

Our fingers touched, my left, his right, our hands like ice.

"And . . ."

"Are we starting?"

"Shut up, Dusty. Of course we're starting."

"I just want to be sure."

His hand was suddenly sweaty. Or maybe mine was.

"Listen," I said, "I'm about to start."

"Okay."

"The next time I say . . . the word."

"And?"

"Yes."

"Okay."

"AND . . ."

I could feel his hand tremble a bit. Mine, too.

"ONE," I said, breathing in loudly.

I could hear him doing the same.

"TWO," I said, difficult to do while holding a breath in. My mouth was wide open. Glancing sideways, I could see Dusty's great gape.

"THREE!" I said.

The Shout whooshed out of me, again burning my tongue, my lips. But this time, it didn't feel as if I'd thrown up hot ginger tea, because Dusty's Shout was doubling mine. Instead, it felt as if the Shout were made of pulped ginger pouring out of me. Volcanic, pure heat. Burned lips. Scorched throat.

At the same time, I made the Wish. I didn't even pause to set it in rhyme.

I wish the great Gate would separate itself from the rock and all its magick melt away. I wish that the great Gate before us would fall away from us, making a walkway into the corridor ahead. I wish that we would be free and all that holds us here be gone.

The twinned Shouts bounced off the rock walls, echoed off the rock floor, rebounded off the rock ceiling, quadrupling back on themselves, over and over and over again, till the two of us were like finely pulled lines vibrating in tune. My body trembled, my hair trembled, my heart trembled. It was *that* kind of Shout.

Then slowly, very slowly, the echoes died away and all around us was as silent as a tomb.

For long moments, I heard nothing. Not a breath, not a sigh, not a sob.

And then, I heard a great, deep moan, as if the very stones were in agony. It felt as if the stone beneath us and all the stone above us had begun to shift. Rocks fell, crashing loudly around us, a waterfall of them.

I wanted to move, to run away, back to where the two princes and the tribe cowered in safety. But my feet seemed stuck to the moving stones. My limbs would not listen to what my mind told them to do.

Closing my eyes, I clutched Dusty's cold, wet, trembling

hand. We clung together, fingers interlaced, making whimpering noises, like whipped dogs.

When the groaning stone finally stopped moving, I opened my eyes again.

There were fissures in the rocks around the Gate, as if a giant with a great sword had tried to split them in two and failed.

But the Gate had not moved at all.

·13·

AFTER THE SHOUT

"What happened?" Dusty asked. "Gorse, what's happened here?"

"*Nothing* has happened here but a lot of stupid noise," I said angrily, exhausted by the terror and the unrhymed Wish. My lips were sore, my throat raw, my head was aching again, and all for nothing. *Nothing!*

"How can that be?"

I turned and yelled at him, "How should *I* know? It's only the second Real Shout I've ever made in my life, and the first one worked." I bit my lip. It had worked only too well, but I hadn't meant to tell him that.

"Then what's the difference?"

I looked back at the Gate. It seemed to be laughing at me. Then I turned and saw a fine gray dust in my brother's hair, on his shoulders, a sparkling kind of dust that caught the light from the hearth.

Stone dust.

That's when I understood.

"Magick," I said. "Much older magick than our Shout. Much stronger. Our poor magick won't bring *that* Gate down. Not now. Not ever. It'll bring the walls down on us first."

Quickly, then, I told him everything I'd left out. I explained all about the Curse, and the imprisonment, and how we were related to both men. And then I told him about the Oath I'd been forced to take, and he let out a fearsome swear.

"Mab's backside!"

I slapped a hand over his mouth. "We have enough trouble down here without you stirring up the Old Ones."

"Whosh, little sister. What have you gotten yourself into?" He collapsed onto the stone floor, folded his legs, and said nothing else for a full minute.

Slowly, I lowered myself down next to him, so exhausted I could hardly move without falling over. My head wasn't just aching; it seemed on fire. I didn't mean to, but I began to weep.

Dusty put an arm around my shoulder. "Don't cry, little

Goose. A Real Shout *is* tiring. No wonder we can only do one a day." He giggled. "And some of us are done for a week or more after. Why, Aunt Gardenia once took to her bed for a full month having given a great Shout, or so Solange said. Not"—he raised his left hand to forestall what was sure to be my next comment—"that I believe everything Solange tells me."

"Hush," I whispered to him, snuffling up the rest of the tears. "Don't say that aloud. I don't want the princes to know."

"Know what?"

"How often we can . . . you know."

"Shout?" He whispered it.

I nodded.

"Ah . . ." He smiled and put a finger to his lips. "Silence is the word." As if Dusty could ever be silent about anything. But he *could* find the humor in just about any situation.

"Promise?"

"I promise."

It wasn't as binding as an Oath, but then I'd never ask that of him. I had to trust him to do the right thing. He was my brother, after all.

For a moment, my traitor mind went to the other brothers whose actions had led us to this place—Orybon and

Fergus. *They* were to blame, not Dusty or me. We were Shouting Fey, and generations removed from them. It was not the same at all.

But then I shook myself back into honesty. It wasn't only *their* fault. I'd gotten into this mess all on my own, because of my rushing about, choosing the easiest route to the castle against all prohibitions, and because of my accident-prone nature. Also because I didn't think things through carefully enough. And by my actions, I'd brought Dusty into the mess, too.

"I'm so sorry," I told him, and began weeping all over again. When he tried to protest, I added, "My head hurts, and my throat hurts. I never want to do another Shout again, ever."

And I meant it, too. At the time.

As we sat huddled together in our misery, we realized that the trembling beneath us had stopped. The sound of stone grinding on stone had stopped as well. And that's when a bunch of shadows walked toward us.

"What was *that*?" Prince Orybon asked as soon as he'd reached us. Behind him the McGargles gabbled in their own language, but clearly they were asking the same thing. Only Grey was silent.

"A Shout," said Dusty.

"I know it was a Shout, stupid fey!" The prince reached out and cuffed Dusty on the ear.

"Ow!"

I could see that Dusty was more angry than hurt. His face was scrunched up and furious. No one smacks anyone in the Family. So I said quickly, remembering something I'd read in a book on the *E* shelf, "It's called an *earthquake,* prince."

"Explain." Now that he had Dusty to bang about and bully, he was no longer wasting more words on me than needed.

As best I could—my head throbbing with the remnants of the Shout and the Gate's ward against it—I explained about plates moving on top of one another, which created fissures and tremors and tremblors and . . .

"Are you just making this up?" Prince Orybon's voice was hard as stone.

"Why would I do that?" I tried to sound astonished that he'd believe any such thing. But even to my own ears, that explanation of an earthquake sounded more like a table setting gone bad. And of course he knew I'd been holding back about my name and the Family all along, so I expect he'd a right to ask. "I read about it in my Father's library."

"I *never* believe what I read in libraries," he said. "You

can't bring any pressure to bear on books, or question them, so how do you know they are truthful?"

It was clear how much he liked bringing pressure. I thought about the pressure he'd put on me, and on Grey, and how we'd been made to do his Bidding the way the Family has to do the human king's. Poor Grey had carried his burden for centuries.

"Why would a book lie?" I asked.

He gave me a withering look. "I suppose it depends who wrote the thing, doesn't it?"

I supposed he had a point.

So Dusty and I went with the prince and Grey to examine the walls on either side of the Gate, but were very careful not to get so close as to set off the sparks again. The McGargles stayed far behind.

The fissures and slices had not changed in the few minutes since Dusty and I'd examined them, and Dusty made the mistake of saying so. He received an angrier cuff on the other ear in answer.

"Maybe another Shout?" Grey suggested.

"Of course another Shout," Prince Orybon said.

Dusty turned and glared at him. "We're too exhausted from that one," he said quickly. "And G—"

I nudged him with my elbow in case he said my real name. He understood at once.

"*My sister* hurt her voice and her head. She needs to rest up if you want the next Shout to work."

"How long?" Orybon asked, glaring back at Dusty, hand raised.

Grey stepped between them and put his hands up in supplication. "We have all the time in the world, prince," he reminded. Then looked back at me and winked.

He's guessed . . . I thought. *Somehow he's guessed we can only do one Shout a day, and he hasn't said anything about it to the prince. Curiouser and curiouser.*

Prince Orybon chuckled and waved Grey away dismissively. "Let them rest, then. They are just children."

"As you wish." Grey head-bobbed and turned away, quickly shepherding Dusty and me away from the prince. He led us back through the maze of tunnels to a nearby cavern half the size of the one where he and the prince usually stayed. In this one stood a large bed by the hearth, twice as big as the pink-and-gold bed I'd been sleeping on, with draperies hung all around to keep it snug. It filled almost every inch of the smaller cavern.

"Where did they get . . . " Dusty began, his eyes suddenly grown big.

"Oh, for pity's sake," I said, sounding like one of the Aunts. "It's a *glamour*."

"Oh." His disappointment showed on his face as if he

really were a child and not nearly fifteen years old. At a calmer, less fraught time, he would have laughed and made a joke at his own expense, but there was no joking here.

Glamour or not, the bed was comfortable, and we *were* exhausted. We fell asleep, and I had the same dream as before—chimera, gray knight, crown, throne, door, and a burst of stars.

I woke up screaming, "Shout! Shout! Shout!" as if I were in the midst of an ague-ridden nightmare.

Dusty woke at my screams and wrapped his arms around me, the way Father would have done. He smoothed down my startled hair. "It's all right, Goosling," he crooned. "I'm here."

Comforted, I fell back to sleep at once.

When I woke, parched, there was a cup of cold river water by the bed, but Dusty wasn't there. He was sitting with Grey on two small, smoothed-down stalagmites halfway across the cavern, deep in conversation.

Getting up from the bed of moss, cup in hand, I sipped it slowly while walking gingerly over to them. I was trying to keep my poor pounding head from hurting even more. "Don't start any new plans without me," I said, my voice scratchy.

They looked up like guilty boys and gave me almost identical grins. It was as if I could see the thirteen-year-old that Grey had once been. Clearly, he'd been under Orybon's thumb for far too long, and we—whether or not we could bring down the Gate—had already changed his life and given him back a kind of innocence.

Grey said, "We have fish for breakfast or . . . *fish* for breakfast."

That made me laugh, much too loudly and much too long for so feeble a joke. Oddly enough, I hardly noticed my headache after that.

"I'll take . . . fish," I said, and he handed me his stone plate and what remained on it.

"That's it?"

He nodded. "But next time I see a passing McGargle, I'll ask for more."

"Move over," I told Dusty, and he moved, leaving me a corner of the stone to sit on. I ate the offered fish ravenously, while they continued to talk. That the fish was cold, and left over from Grey's breakfast, didn't matter. I only held myself back from licking the plate out of a sense of embarrassment. But if I'd been alone, I would have licked it in an instant.

They continued their conversation, heedless of my manners. Actually, it was less a conversation than an odd argument. Grey was holding forth on fey battles, and Dusty was explaining about the building of stone walls. Less an argument than a pair of monologues, each one fascinating in its own way.

I waded in with my own. "I had a dream . . . " I began.

"Don't pay her any attention," Dusty said, shaking his head. He smiled wryly at Grey. "She *always* has dreams. Wild dreams, improbable dreams. Possibly prophetic dreams, or so the Aunts think, though none of the dreams have ever come true."

"All dreams are wild, improbable, and possibly prophetic," Grey said. "That's the nature of dreams. Perhaps no one has been reading them aright."

I think my mouth gaped wide.

"Don't encourage her," Dusty said, clearly wanting to get back to talk of battles and stone walls.

Ignoring Dusty's warning, Grey leaned in toward me. "Tell me the dream."

"Really?" I tried to fathom his reason for asking.

"*Really,*" he said in such a reasonable fashion, I did.

As I told it, I think I understood the dream for the first time, reading it *aright* myself, as Grey suggested. "I thought it meant I had to throw a Shout at the Gate, but we all saw how that came out."

"Gate one, fey nil," Dusty joked, making it sound as if the Shout were only a boy's game. And maybe for him it was. He hadn't taken an Oath, after all. At least not yet.

"Not *nil* at all," Grey said. "We have gotten something from the Shout."

"Nothing *I* can see," said Dusty.

"Then you are not looking hard enough." Grey was no longer the boy, but a teacher of boys.

Suddenly, understanding what Grey meant, I leaned forward with excitement. "We *learned* something."

Grey smiled at me. "A battle lost is not a war lost, as long as the losing side takes good information away from the encounter."

"Exactly!" I'd seen that very sentence in *The Book of Battles* by the Greek writer Athenios, a huge tome I'd found on the *B* shelf and read a bit of one sunny afternoon in the meadow. I remembered it specifically because the meadow seemed such an unlikely place to read such a book, and I only understood a small part of what I found in the book. I liked the stories of the particular battles best, not the parts about battle strategy. But that sentence Grey quoted, coming at the end of one disastrous battle whose armies I couldn't recall, had made an impression on me. "Athenios," I said, and when Grey looked startled that I knew it, I grinned broadly.

"My, my, you *are* a surprise," he said.

Dusty laughed. "Father always says that about her," he told Grey.

But I thought that it was Grey who'd been the surprise.

Dusty suddenly realized something and shook his head. "What information did we get?"

Grey said, "Do you want to tell him, or shall I?"

"I will," I said, putting my hand on Dusty's. "The Gate didn't fall, but some of the wall around it crumbled."

"So?"

"So . . ." I prompted.

"So . . . another Shout?" he guessed.

"And another," I said. "And another. Until it's done."

"Or *we're* done," Dusty warned.

He was right, of course. We Shouters all had to rest after a Shout, some—it seems—more than others. I more than most.

"But *surely* we have plenty of time," I said. "And a wall of stone, unlike a wall of ivy, won't grow back." If there was a whine in my voice, I hadn't meant it to be there.

Grey held up a hand to silence us. "The prince has not the patience he once had, and that was little enough. Now that we are so close to the end of this exile—or so he hopes—he wants everything done and over."

"Don't you want it done and over, too?" I watched a series of emotions race across his handsome face as he formed his answer.

"I want it done properly, and with no loss of life—to

us, to the McGargles, to anyone. But Orybon just wants it done fast. He would have made a terrible general."

I nodded.

Grey crossed his arms and looked at Dusty and me, as if he was about to say something that was heresy, and it was. "Prince Orybon no longer has his great magicks, which may be due to the exile, his father's Curse, or the closeness of the Gate, which is why we stay mostly as far from this part of the cave as is possible. But I have seen him still work small Curses on some of the tribe. It is never a pretty sight. I would not have him hurt the two of you."

"Why should we trust what *you* say?" asked Dusty, his face getting that pinched look that shows he is worried.

Though it may sound strange, given what I'd been through with Grey, I *did* trust him, and said so. "Because he has no reason now to lie."

Dusty stood up. His hands in fists struck against his thighs. His anger exploded from his clothing in stone dust that our sleep hadn't erased. "Don't be stupid, Gorse. *Of course* he has a reason. He's the prince's man."

I hissed at him, saying my name like that, calling me stupid, saying what he did about Grey. Though, surprisingly, the only thing I taxed him with was the last. "Grey's under an Oath as binding as mine," I said. "And has been since he was thirteen years old. He doesn't do things for the prince out of love or even out of loyalty, but because he *must,* or he'll be turned into a thousand stars."

In that single moment, Dusty's face went from pinched anger to real compassion. He always flares up and down like that. He sat again and said in a gentled voice, "Then what *do* we do?"

Grey pulled us in by saying confidently, "We read the dream aright. And then we follow its instruction."

"But . . . but . . ." Dusty began, but it was clear his heart was no longer in his protest.

"Tell us the dream again," Grey said, "only more slowly and completely. Leave *nothing* out."

And so I did.

· 14 ·

A FLIGHT OF BATS

It must have been evening by the time we got back to the Gate, for we were suddenly engulfed in a new dark wind whooshing up toward the vaulted ceiling and out through the hole so far above us.

"What's that?" Dusty asked, sounding at once startled and interested.

"Bats," Grey and I said together.

"Does it frighten you, little cousin?" asked Orybon, who seemed to have suddenly become visible, as if he'd been wearing my Cloak, though *it* was bound around my waist and *still* not working. I realized later that the prince must have just been leaning against the wall and staring at the Gate, and we'd passed by him without noticing. Not magick after all.

"Bats don't scare me," said Dusty, pinched face half turned to glare at the prince.

"But *I* should," Orybon said.

"You're trying to sound like the villain in a faerie tale," I pointed out. "But Dusty and I have both heard enough of those to know what happens to such folk. Red-hot iron shoes, barrels full of snakes, and—"

"Pushed into an oven," Grey added.

"This is *not* a children's tale," Orybon said petulantly, and then must have thought better of his tone, and laughed. It was a forced sound and not particularly pleasant, but it served to make him seem reasonable again.

To Dusty.

Not to me.

"Cousin," Grey put in smoothly, "the children and I have been trying to come up with a plan."

I noticed—and so did Prince Orybon—that Grey was no longer addressing him as a ruling master. I smiled at that, but Orybon's lips thinned out, and he positively simmered with anger.

"The simplest thing is to let them Shout again," Orybon said, once more using his dry voice.

"It is not . . . as *simple* as that," Grey said.

"Seems simple enough to me," the prince told him. "If one of their bedamned Shouts has loosened some rocks, a second Shout will undoubtedly loosen even more."

So he'd noticed that as well. I wasn't sure if this was good news or bad.

Grey went over to him, holding out his hands, palms up as if making a peace offering. "You have two weapons, my prince. But they are fragile. Too many Shouts and they will be broken lances in your hands: pretty objects, but useless. However—"

"How me no evers." The prince's voice hardened. It was like the stone that surrounded us.

But Grey had been with him too long to be cowed by such tricks. "In Oberon's name, my prince, stop being stupid about this and listen. We have time. It is both our Curse and our salvation. We have weapons—these fey Shouters." He pointed to us. "*And* . . ." He prolonged the word till Orybon could not help but be reeled in. "We have a girl who dreams prophetic dreams."

Orybon's eyes widened at the mention of the dreams, but Grey didn't say anything more, not that there was much more to say. He waited to let the prince become interested on his own. Clearly Grey knew when to lead and when to be led.

Orybon leaned in. "What about those dreams?"

I suddenly realized I was holding my breath.

"Let us read those dreams, my prince," Grey said, "to find out what more we need to do to make these walls come down safely *and* in a reasonable amount of time."

"This is not a *joke*?"

"No."

"Not more of your folderol and storytelling?"

"No."

"Then show me the *evidence* of these dreams." Orybon's mouth was hard again, like stone.

Grey shrugged, held up his hands in mock surrender, then turned and walked back toward us, saying over his shoulder, "Sometimes, my prince, faith is more powerful than evidence."

"I am hardly a model for faithfulness," said the prince, trying hard to disguise his interest. He followed Grey, strolling along as if that interest had not been piqued. But I knew better, for why else would he be following Grey? And Grey knew, too. Orybon wouldn't have moved a foot otherwise.

Dusty made a *harrumph* sound through his nose, rather like a disgruntled horse. He thought the prince didn't care, but he was wrong.

"Tell him," Grey instructed as we stood six or seven feet from the Gate. Close enough to encourage us, far enough not to spit out fire.

By this time, some of the McGargles had also crept closer, including the hairless one. How much they understood what was going on, I didn't know, though the one without the hair seemed to be doing the most explaining, almost as though he was able to understand our language and translate it into theirs. Later Grey explained it even more thoroughly to them in their own language. The prince didn't. Either, like the Family's king, he disdained speaking to peasants, or he'd never learned their tongue.

I said, "We need more than simple Shouts."

Orybon said, "I thought there was nothing simple about them."

I said, "We need something to throw at the dam."

He said, "What is she gabbling about?"

Dusty laughed. "Maybe if you'd just listen . . ." Now he finally understood we'd gotten Orybon's interest.

I said quickly, to soften Dusty's insult, "The human king of our country, prince, made a bathing spot for his queen and her maidens by damming up a river near us. Though my brothers and boy cousins liked watching the girls as they bathed, they liked the flowing river even better. So they tried a *simple* Shout to break the dam. First one, then another, then the rest of the boys tried Shouting together. The water riffled and rippled and splashed and spilled over its banks, but the dam was too well built and the boys' Shouts too unpracticed."

Orybon said, "Get to the point."

I said, "This *is* the point."

Grey said, "You think, cousin, that you are subtle, but this girl is more subtle than you will ever be."

Dusty laughed.

The prince slapped him.

Dusty laughed again, then easily ducked the next slap, at which Orybon growled, something I would've expected from an animal or a McGargle, not a prince. Not *that* particular prince at any rate.

"Tell him," Dusty said, not a command, but a plea. "Now!"

"My brothers couldn't Shout down the dam, so they Shouted the upstream river down. Along with all its float of tree trunks and broken boats and the leftovers from a year of winter ice storms." I didn't tell him that was a day later, and after Father had coached them in what to do.

Grey said, "The river did the work for them, you see."

Orybon said, "This is madness. Just Shout the Cursed Gate down."

I said, "That's not what the dream told me to do."

Dusty added, "We're going to make the stone work for us. Since we *can't* destroy the Gate itself. It's got a lot bigger magick than we have. We'll let the stone drag it down for us."

Orybon said, "*That,* at least, makes sense. Perhaps I've been hitting the wrong sibling." He walked away from us into the dark.

Dusty turned to Grey. "Is he *always* like this?"

"Sometimes worse."

The three of us laughed. It felt liberating to laugh that way, even when it rose into a kind of hysteria.

After a while, we stopped laughing and got down to the hard part. The explosion part.

"The dam example is all very well and good," said Grey, looking steadily at both of us, "but in actuality, it was never as dangerous as what we are about to try."

"Why?" Dusty asked. "Water or stone, they both need moving, and can both kill you if handled badly."

"Brother, I love you dearly," I said to him, "but the dammed-up water in that pool wasn't enough to drown anyone. It would have just overflowed its banks if you boys had made a mistake. However, if we aren't careful here, there's a lot of stone going to come down onto our heads."

Grey's right hand suddenly banged down on top of his left. "*Bam!*" he shouted.

Dusty flinched.

"And," I added, "we need more than a few Shouts. We need—"

"Something explosive." Dusty nodded, looking around the Gate cave. "Like Father's skyrockets. Okay, I get it. But—"

“There is a beetle,” Grey said pensively. “It explodes fire and acid at its stalkers.”

“I’ve read about it,” I said. “Agrippa. He wrote about natural magick. He said that the beetle explosions are like the way a unicorn’s horn purifies water.”

Grey shook his head. “I have seen no such beetles in the cave.”

“And we don’t believe in unicorns,” Dusty said.

“Do you not?” A smile played across Grey’s face.

“Speaking of reading . . . I’ve got an idea,” I said. “Something I saw in a book last year. About bats.”

“Bats explode?” Dusty looked puzzled. “Sister, you read the strangest books. That can warp your mind.”

“Expand her mind, rather,” countered Grey, but to me, not to Dusty.

“No, bats don’t explode, but there’s something in their . . . their . . .” I made a motion with my hand, pointing behind me.

“Guano,” said Grey.

“Poo,” I said at the same time.

“You *must* be joking.” Dusty tried to laugh, but there seemed to be no laugh left in him.

I shrugged. “Well, that’s what I read.”

“Which part?” asked Dusty. “Which part of the guano poo are we talking about?”

“I . . . I don’t know. It just said it was . . . used for making explosives." I hesitated. "Like Father's skyrockets. Only not a toy. More powerful."

"His skyrockets aren't made of poo. The exploding part's not mushy at all." Dusty was looking disgusted and waving his hands about.

"Well, ours won't be mushy either," Grey said in a sensible voice as he moved toward a far wall. "Cannon powder, even back in my day, was always dry. So, let's do an experiment."

"Where are you—" I began.

"Going?" finished Dusty.

"To get some really tall McGargles to help in the harvest." His voice threaded back to us, echoing off the cave walls.

"Harvest?" I stared after him.

"Of guano," he called back. "From the cave walls."

I started after him, stopped, turned to Dusty, waved him forward. "Come on!" I said.

"Absolutely not!"

"Dusty!"

"No!"

But in the end, of course, he came. It wasn't brotherly love that brought him along, but plain, old-fashioned Dusty curiosity.

After Grey had talked to the tallest members of the Tribe, the hairless one led them off to do the harvesting. Since they had no real tools except for a few stone scrapers, I expected that it would take some time, though it turned out they were dedicated and quick workers, especially once Grey had convinced them that this was a plan to get them all released from the cave.

Once they were gone, we three hunkered down by the hearth near where Dusty and I had so recently slept. There was no glamour on the bed—it was not moss, only a pile of hair. McGargle hair, at a guess. Goodness only knew what fleas and bugs inhabited it. I began to feel itchy just thinking about it. And the guano.

And of course my head still ached. But that was the least of my worries.

"First," Grey was saying, "we have to take stock of what we have."

"Stones," Dusty said.

"Unhelpful." I scratched at my hair, then forced myself to stop itching.

"Everything is helpful at this stage," Grey reminded us. But he winked at me, so I'd know he wasn't scolding.

"Guano," I said, making a face.

"And fire." Dusty pointed at the hearth where the fire made soft cracking noises.

Grey nodded. "And the oyl that feeds it. Plus my tinderbox." He pulled at a leather thong around his neck and at the end was a silver tinderbox that had been hidden beneath his shirt and tunic. "My father gave it to me when I was a boy, before they sent me off to the Unseelie Court as a hostage, and I have never parted from it."

"And your sword," said Dusty, nodding at the sheathed weapon.

"Good." Grey nodded.

"Fish and fish bones," I said, recalling our meals. Then I remembered something else. "My spindle." I didn't mention the Cloak of Invisibility. It really had no bearing on any explosion and—besides—it still wasn't working.

"Bedstead," Dusty said, then looked around and for the first time really saw the pile where the glamoured bed had been. "Or whatever that is."

"Hair," said Grey. "We shear the grown-up McGargles once a year, or they'd be unable to see or walk with any comfort. Evidently out in the world, they had special trees they rubbed against, but that knowledge is useless to them here. If we didn't shear them once a year, we would be unable to stand very close to them." He sniffed.

"What do you use?" Dusty asked suspiciously.

Grey reached into his boot and drew out a long dagger.

"So we have a dagger, too." Dusty smiled, touching the sharp point. He was the Family's mumblety-peg champion. But there was no earth here on which to play the game, only stone that would blunt the knife's end.

"And our Shouts," I said. Then shrugged. "If those can help."

"We don't know yet *what* can help," said Grey.

"That's it," I said.

"That's it," Dusty concurred.

Grey nodded. "That *is* it."

"Bats," I said, as a final afterthought. "Beetles, slugs, worms?" Though I hadn't seen any.

Grey had nothing left to say. Dusty was silent as well.

So, I shut up, too, thinking instead about the list of the few—the *very* few—things we had to work with. The silence was only broken by the hearth fire, which snapped at us like a petulant prince. Its tongue-lashing seemed the perfect complement to our mood.

Suddenly, as if summoned by the fire, Orybon appeared. His ability to do so was beginning to wear on me. If the Cloak had been working, I'd have given him a taste of True Invisibility he wouldn't soon forget. But the silly thing still hung grimly around my waist like an unwanted guest at a banquet.

"Are we having a meeting or a snore?" he asked, gesturing with the spindle.

"We're considering options," said Grey. His tone was sharp and his face sharper.

"And I was not invited?" Orybon glared down at us.

"You walked out on us," I said.

"Pull up a stone and sit down with the peasants," Dusty told him cheekily, almost inviting another cuff to the ear.

But this time, Orybon didn't try to slap Dusty. He seemed somehow less sure of himself than before. Or less angry. Perhaps he'd been thinking about explosions on his own. Or settling his stomach. Or considering dreams and faith. He did sit down, though, close enough to Dusty to make me uneasy, but far enough from me to give me hope.

"Have you managed to come up with anything even *resembling* a plan?" he asked. "Or have you spent the time trading more dreams and family reminiscences?"

Well, perhaps not *less* angry after all!

"We, dear cousin . . . " began Grey.

"I was speaking to *Pudding Alice*."

So the order of where we all stood with Prince Orybon had changed. Evidently, Grey could no longer serve him as well as I could, and that made me fear for Grey.

"The *three* of us," I said carefully, "are thinking about explosives. And as Prince Grey has more ideas on that subject than I do . . ." I left that idea hanging and turned my back on the prince, looking instead at Grey, who knew exactly what I was doing. He gave me a genuine smile, and again I could almost see the boy in him, the one who first came into the Unseelie Court all alone, innocent, and easily manipulated by a cunning, older, angry prince.

• • • • • • • •

"Explosions! How is that different from a Shout?" Orybon's voice rose.

Grey said quietly, "As different as lightning is to a lightning bug."

I suppressed a giggle.

"If you know so much about explosions, *cousin* . . ." Orybon's voice got dangerously low and quiet. "Then why have we not blown up that bedamned Gate before now?"

"Because, as you know, we cannot get near enough to the Gate, and I didn't know what I now know about how to make the power I need to blow up the rocks around the Gate."

"Because of these two?"

Grey nodded. "Because of these two." He smiled, adding, "And because of Pudding Alice's dream."

"And what is the magickal missing ingredient you found?" Orybon's voice dripped with sarcasm.

Just then the first of the tribe appeared, carrying armfuls of stuff that smelled worse than they did. They dumped it in front of Prince Orybon.

Orybon jumped up and stepped back from the piles. "What *is* that?"

"Bat poo," said Dusty with a ferocious grin. He dipped his hand into the crumbling stuff and held it toward Prince Orybon's face. "Want some?"

Orybon turned on his heel and made a hasty retreat into the darkness.

"Did you have to do that?" I asked.

"How could I not?" Dusty's grin was a league wide.

Laughing uproariously, Grey tumbled backward off his stalagmite seat and landed bottom first on the stone floor.

We spent the next few hours experimenting, using the handle of Grey's knife and several rocks to pound the guano into a grayish powder. Afterward, we set little bits of it alight with a torch made from the shorn McGargle hair held aloft on the sword and bound with my ribbon.

The smell of the burning hair was almost as bad as the guano. But the powder burned with a lovely lilac flame and then exploded with a loud *pop*. Each time we tried, we got another small explosion. These were tiny, short, and sharp, but nothing exactly powerful. Still, we understood we were onto something real. It worked and was repeatable.

Dusty danced about like a loon when the first bit of powder popped. And when the second and third did, Grey joined him. They were like two boys seeing their first sky-rockets.

Next we tried making a paste of some of the powder with water from the river, stirring it with the largest fish bones we could find. Grey forbade us the use of his knife for that. The watery guano turned to glop that looked a great deal like something a cow might have dropped onto the stone floor. It wouldn't ignite at all.

"So now we know it has to be the powder form," said Grey. Dusty and I agreed.

"How much guano are we going to need?" Dusty asked.

"A great deal more if we are to make a large explosion," Grey told him. "But the McGargles are in charge of that. So we need not worry."

"And how are we going to make the kind of explosion we need?" I asked. "We daren't get too close to light it ourselves else we'll be blown up."

Grey got a strange look on his face. "Orybon will probably suggest using a McGargle."

"Oh, no!" I said, suddenly remembering the death of poor old Gargle. "We can't do that."

"Of course not," said Grey. "We need some sort of fuse."

"What's a fuse?" Dusty and I asked together.

"It is what initiates the actual explosion, a kind of cord that leads away from the powder to a place where we can be safe. We light the far end, and the fire travels along the cord until at last it reaches the great residue of powder. Then BOOM!" His voice sent thrills of echoes running through the cavern.

"Oh, that," Dusty said, disgusted. "We call it a string." He cocked his head at Grey. "For our rockets. Of course, those are short . . ."

"Short fuses for small explosions," Grey said, "and long fuses . . ."

"I get it," Dusty said.

"I like the word *fuse*," I said, trying to close down any argument before it started. But I was not convinced a fuse could work. "What could we possibly make the cord out of?"

"A piece of excess clothing," Grey explained, eyeing the Cloak around my waist.

"Not that!" I said, shielding it as best I could with my hands. "It's . . . it's . . ."

"It's what?" He leaned toward me. There was a kind of gleam in his eye that made me doubt him all over again. After all, he'd been in the cave for uncounted dreary years. Being around Orybon all that time *must* have rubbed off on him.

Dusty said, "It's her traveling cloth. She sleeps with it and always has it somewhere near to hand." Dusty's voice was rough with the lie, but only I noticed.

The Magick Gods' blessings on you, brother. I looked at the floor of the cave so Grey couldn't read my face.

"Then," Grey said, "we shall use *my* shirt. I still have a doublet to keep me warm."

"And the hearth fire," I whispered.

"And the glamour," Dusty added. Though we all knew that a glamour couldn't actually warm you, just make you *look* warm.

Grey sent the McGargles out to get more, and more, and then even more of the guano till we had huge piles of the stuff everywhere. He and Dusty took turns smashing it into dust while I had the job of pulling Grey's shirt apart, plaiting the threads into a long, thin, pliable rope that would become our fuse.

·15·

CURSES

It took us three days. Or at least it took us three times between sleep periods before we were ready, all marked by the whoosh of the bats out of the cave. Whether that was time as calculated Under the Hill or over, I couldn't be sure, though it had to be long after the christening. But I couldn't bring myself to dwell on that. And as Dusty and I were still alive and not turned into stardust, I was at least slightly comforted.

The McGargles had several rough-made willow baskets, probably from their days before they'd been closed up in the caves. We loaded the powder into those for transportation to the walls on either side of the Gate. But not too near, lest sparks from the Gate ignite the powder before we were ready.

"Careful, careful . . ." Grey cautioned us, and then in the McGargle tongue cautioned them as well.

The McGargles were only as cautious as large trolls can be, but they avoided going up close to the Gate because they were terrified of it. Only once did one of the baby trolls get too close. It probably wanted to play with the guano dust. But its mother—or father—raced over and hauled it back. The little one complained in a high-pitched squeal all the way. The grown-up's hair started to burn from the Gate's orange sparks—the smell was predictably awful—but the others quickly patted it out with their large hands.

Luckily, none of the sparks came close to the growing piles of guano dust, or it might have all been blown up beforetimes, and us with it.

Soon there were two knee-high piles against the stone walls on either side of the Gate, though none closer than about seven feet. Knee-high to an adult McGargle, that is, which put it chest-high on Grey.

Under Grey's direction, the McGargles used the baskets like a farmer's rake to shove the piles closer to the Gate, maybe three feet on either side closer. Then they tidied up the bits of guano dust that had escaped, using their hands, until their hairy arms fairly glittered with the stuff.

"Had enough sparkles, Mr. Magpie?" I asked Dusty as he loaded the last of the guano into the baskets.

"I think," Dusty said, "I've had enough sparkles to last me a lifetime." He wiped his arm over his sweaty brow, leaving a line of dust there, like a girl's hair ribbon. I brushed it off carefully.

Grey turned to me. "Are you ready with the fuse?"

I held up the skinny, snakelike thing to show him. It was longer than two McGargles.

"Good." He took the cord from me and cut it in two with his knife. "One for each pile."

Then he went over to the nearest hearth, which was unlit, and soaked both strands in the oyl. "It should make the cords burn even better," he said, over his shoulder, before coiling each into large greasy ropes. By now his hands were smudged with the black oyl. I could smell him from where I stood and wrinkled my nose, but he never noticed.

Dusty took one of the coils from Grey and set its mouth against the guano powder to the left of the Gate, while Grey set his to the pile on the right.

The McGargles cheered, though once again Grey cautioned them. I think he was afraid that, in their excitement, they might start jumping around and scatter the dust.

After the cheer, Grey and Dusty each unrolled the rest of the two fuses backward toward the corridor where we planned to wait, close enough to be able to hear what was happening, far enough away to be *relatively* safe. They were both filthy with oyl by the time they were done, and stinking as badly as the trolls.

The McGargles crowded in with us, though the corridor was too small for that many, so Grey shooed them farther back, but—even so—the smell of their hairy bodies, combining with the oyl pong on Grey and Dusty, made my headache throb madly. The corridor seemed to glitter and whirl as if I'd been twirling around. Though to be fair, I didn't know if the headache and the strange visions before my eyes were from the smells, from fear, from the nearness of the Gate, or from the residue of magick.

"Now what?" Dusty asked.

"Now," Grey said, "I go to the Gate cave, set both cords alight, and then run back here, where we will wait for the explosions."

"I'm going with you," I said to Grey. The tone of my voice let him know I wouldn't be talked out of it.

"And I!" said Dusty.

Grey shrugged, but a small smile played around his lips, and he couldn't disguise it.

As instructed, the McGargles went galloping and whooping back through the long, twisting corridor, but Dusty and I followed Grey into the Gate cave and stood near the ends of the fuses while Grey prepared to set them on fire. He fiddled with the tinderbox, mumbling something—whether a Curse or a prayer, I couldn't tell. The tinderbox seemed reluctant to light the cords.

"Wait!" I said. "Where's Prince Orybon?"

"Who cares?" Dusty growled.

Grey handed me the tinderbox. "Guard it with your life," he said. The tinderbox was smeared with the oyl, too. I sighed. There was no getting away from that smell now.

Checking the main cavern first, Grey came back shortly to grumble that he'd no idea where Orybon was, but at least he wasn't near the Gate and therefore wasn't in any immediate danger.

"Too bad," Dusty said.

A hand cuffed his ear.

"Ow!"

"If this doesn't work, it will be too bad for *you*," Orybon said, having emerged almost—as it were—from the corridor wall.

"You *could* have said something," Grey told him.

"It was more amusing this way, watching you all work so hard. At least it made the time pass."

I glared at him. "It could have passed even faster if you'd been helping."

"I doubt that."

"I doubt that, too," grumbled Dusty.

"Well," Orybon said, lips pursed as if he'd eaten something sour, "at least we agree on something, little fey." He turned and faced the Gate. For a moment, he stood still as a statue, then said in a loud voice, "I Curse your Gate, Father, and you who made it. I Curse the hands that touched it and turned it against me. I Curse the mind that thought it up. And when I get home—and that *will* be soon, no thanks to you—I shall wrest the throne from your thrice-Cursed, aging body and Curse you again into your grave."

I was shocked.

Dusty was appalled.

"Was that wise?" I asked, not looking at the prince but at Grey, who'd returned in time to hear the prince's entire speech.

Grey shrugged, took the tinderbox back from me. Our fingers touched. I went red with embarrassment, for it felt as if the Gate had shot sparks between the two of us. We glanced at each other, and he had the grace to look away first. "That's what *he* calls repentance," he whispered.

"Sounded like a Curse to me," I said.

"Several," Dusty added.

Grey bent over the two fuses and struck the tinderbox, and this time it flared. He touched it to one fuse and, right after, the other. The cords began to burn quickly and efficiently, heading like small fiery carts along their preset tracks.

"That will do it." Prince Orybon stepped over one cord and walked back past the three of us to wait, as always, in the dark.

We all moved back down the corridor, to join the prince in the dark, protected by a thick wall of stone.

I could hear the little *zzzzing* noises of the fire moving along the fuses, but it seemed like too much time had passed and still there was no explosion. I counted to ten, then twenty, then fifty, and still there was no large *BANG!*

At last I couldn't stand it any longer. Inching past the three of them—Dusty, who whispered my name in warning, and Grey, who reached out an oyly hand to stop me, and Orybon, wherever he was hiding—I walked deliberately to where the tunnel opened into the cavern.

I could see the fuses still burning toward the piles of guano powder, but slowly, as if they'd lost the will to go any farther or faster. I could feel their resistance, their reluctance to set the thing alight. As I'd been making them, the cords had felt strong and competent. When Grey had set them on fire, they'd seemed set and purposeful. But now, traveling along the stone floor toward the piles of gray powder and the walls the powder leaned on, the cords looked vastly too small and too insignificant to start any explosion, the powder too frail to bring down stone, and the Gate too powerful and filled with magick to be moved.

Stepping into the cavern, I took a deep breath and found my center. Then, just as the fuses finally reached the powder, and the powder began to burn with that delicate lilac color I'd seen before, I made the Wish.

"Let the walls on either side
Crumble, tumble, open wide.
Let the Gate fall far from me,
And let all go free. Go free!"

The last two words came out in an unexpected Shout, though it seemed to have little of the power of the Shout with Dusty, none of the burning in my throat and tongue. Rather it leaped from my mouth like a shaft of cold fire, coursing along the ashy cords till it caught up with their own fire at the very end.

I leaned forward to watch, thinking, *Certainly not one of the greatest charms, but workable.* Especially with the Shout at the end. I hadn't any time to come up with a better rhyme or a longer one.

Without warning, there came a terrible, multiplying echo of the Shout, as if my brain had exploded, the sound of it terrifying. I heard the explosion long before I saw it. And long before I realized it wasn't the guano and fuse that had made the noise.

Rather it was the whooshing sound of bats suddenly flying around me, as if they somehow knew what was about to happen. I tried to turn away. I put my hands up to keep the bats out of my hair. I wanted to move to anywhere but where I was, but in that same moment, none of my limbs nor my one good wing seemed to be working. Instead, I was lifted up by the air as if I were no more than a puff of milkweed, but at the same time the air seemed hard as stone.

Then I was tossed end over end until I was sure I would empty my stomach or bang my head, and I couldn't decide which one should come first or hurt less.

As I was trying to figure it all out, a sudden downdraft hurtled me toward the stone floor.

There were terrified screams.

Wild laughter.

Cries.

And some of them came from me.

Seconds, minutes, maybe even an hour later, I realized I was mostly unhurt and safely enfolded in someone's familiar strong arms. I opened my eyes.

"Father?" I asked, thinking I'd just awakened from another ague dream.

"Don't be silly, Gorse," said someone close by. "It's the hairless troll. He caught you. You were falling faster than one of Father's skyrockets and he plucked you from the air."

It took me a moment to remember where I was, what a hairless troll was, even who *I* was. Then I looked into the monster's yellow eyes that were narrowing as they focused on me. Without thinking, I whispered, "Gargle?"

He burbled back at me. "Gargle McGargle."

I was astonished. It seems I hadn't killed him after all, just shorn him in the most efficient and permanent way by burning his hair off with my spell.

Something inside me, some wet and weepy thing, some stone wall of guilt, crumbled away. And then, remembering the other crumbling stone, I stuttered hoarsely, "The . . . the . . . Gate?"

Dusty pointed dramatically to a spot behind me. "Look!"

I squirmed out of Gargle's arms and turned to look. It wasn't easy to see through the scrim of rock dust that still filled the cavern. But once my eyes adjusted to the gray light, I saw that on both sides of the Gate, about five feet on either side, where the guano dust had been shoved, the rocks were jagged, broken, tumbling down.

But the Gate itself still stood upright.

"It stands," Prince Orybon said in that dry voice, filled now with an ultimate bitterness. "You have failed me, Pudding Alice, Mistress Goosey, daughter of the Shouting Fey. I wonder that you have not burst into a thousand stars. You swore a binding Oath to me, after all. And failed."

“But not to Shout down the Gate,” Grey reminded him. “Only to deliver your message of repentance to your father.”

“It still stands,” I whispered, not knowing if I meant the Gate or the Oath or maybe both. And also not knowing if somewhere, somehow, Orybon’s father—my Great-grandfather Fergus’s father—*was* still alive to receive a message from me about his son. At that moment, I was too exhausted from the events, my head ached too much from the Shout and its residual magick, and my throat was too raw from the rock dust and my screams to care.

Dusty laughed. “There’s room enough on either side to sidle through, prince. That is, if you aren’t too high and mighty to sidle. Or too afraid of a few minor sparks.”

At that, Orybon shoved the spindle at me and gave Dusty such a cuff, he fell to the stone floor. As if intent on proving Dusty wrong about his fear, Orybon stepped forward. He hadn’t got very far when he was stopped by Grey’s hand on his shoulder.

“Do not go there until I have tried it myself, my prince.”

Still stung by Dusty’s challenge, perhaps even so eager to leave the cave he dismissed all considerations of safety, Orybon shrugged off Grey’s hand and continued forward.

“I am coming, Father!” he cried. “I am coming, Fergus! I am coming back to Curse you all again and again and again. And the worst Curses will be for you, Maeve, you baggage, you blemish, you wanton who broke my heart.”

"What heart?" Dusty muttered.

Suddenly Orybon was running headlong toward the Gate with Grey, the Oath-man, but a step behind.

"Grey!" I cried, heading after them, though as I ran I could feel myself shaking with an ague. Or something like ague.

"Leave them," Dusty said, his hand grabbing mine and stopping me in my tracks. I tried to break free, but he held me fast.

By then, the two princes had gotten to the opening, with Orybon turned sideways, his back against the broken stone to the left of the Gate, inching along toward the corridor on the other side, heedless of all the sparks.

With a terrible, dark growling sound, the Gate itself began to tremble as if it—and not I—had the ague.

Grey had just entered the narrow passage as the Gate's tremors became stronger, more pronounced. It swayed from side to side, seeking the support of the stone that was no longer there to hold it up. The growling sound got louder, scarier.

I could see Grey's hand extending toward Orybon, seeking to grab him and haul him back out, when the whole of the wall on either side of the Gate burst outward, and the two men were carried upward in a kind of magick vortex, like a windstorm. Around and around it spun them before slamming Orybon to the ground, where he began bursting into a thousand stars and—at the same time—was buried beneath a cascade of stone. Quickly, the stone entombed him till not one of the stars could be seen.

Grey remained caught in the swirl, left spinning high up in the air. He made not a sound as he was whipped around and around. Standing far below, we were helpless to reach him and could only watch as he was stripped by the vortex of everything that we recognized as him, before the stone dust stirred up by the cruel wind obscured all.

As if released from a spell, the McGargles all began crying out at once, a great gabble of sound, a howl that was part celebration and part mourning song.

"Gone?" I whispered to Dusty. "Just like that, they're gone?"

"Gone," he said, scrubbing the dust from his eyes.

"The Gate's Curse worked, then. Without true repentance, Orybon wasn't released. And without fulfilling his Oath, Grey . . ." I couldn't say the words.

"Looks like it."

I snuffled. My nose was running now, as well as my eyes. I felt bereft, and I didn't understand why.

"But Grey *kept* his Oath," I whined. "It's not fair."

Dusty's lips were pursed as if he'd been sucking on something sour. "Orybon wasn't worth it. Grey needn't have bothered."

"Grey was the kind of man who would *always* keep an Oath," I said. "He's gone because he went to help the prince."

Dusty nodded and put his arm around me. I could feel him shaking, or maybe it was me shaking. At that moment, I couldn't be sure.

The McGargles' ululations increased behind us until I could hardly hear myself think. I turned and shouted, "I thought you *hated* the prince!" before realizing they were weeping for Grey, as was I.

"What is all the crying about?" a boy's voice asked.

I turned to Dusty, but he wasn't the one talking. Instead he was staring wildly at the Gate, where a slightly familiar-looking boy about his size—but about my age—had suddenly appeared. He seemed a bit dazed, unsure of himself, and was wearing a jacket and trews that were much too big for him. Only his boots seemed to fit.

Dusty understood before I did. "Grey?"

The boy cocked his head to one side. "You know my name?" He was practically tripping over the trews. And I could see a set of grayish bat wings peeking above the jacket's collar.

"We both do," I said, understanding in that moment that Grey—who'd been thirteen when he was tricked into his Oath—had somehow been returned to that age. Somehow sent back to that moment just as the Oath-maker had burst into the stars. The vortex released by the fall of the Gate hadn't killed him at all, but rather had stripped him of his cave age.

I suddenly hoped that I might be released back to the moment I'd taken my Oath about five days ago. But I'd kept my memory intact, perhaps because I hadn't gone up in the spinning winds.

And, not surprising at all, with the fall of the Gate, my headache had almost entirely disappeared.

Grinning at the boy, who was still staring all about him, I said, "It's a long story, Grey, but a good one."

I turned to Dusty, holding the spindle high. "It's time we all went home. There's a christening to get to, and an adoption to see to."

"You are way ahead of me, Gorse," Dusty said.

But then, I always am.

Part III

RECIPE FOR A SPELL

A pinch of thought grated fine,
Some well-plucked words, a rack of rhyme,
Topped with herbs, and then you spin
All to be done widdershin.
Count to three or seven, nine,
And then your spell will turn out fine.

·16·

THE CHRISTENING

Dusty flew me with my one good wing high up over the fallen Gate, setting me down deep inside the farther tunnel. Quickly, he returned to get the bewildered young Grey, whose new-returned wings were still too weak and crumpled to be trusted.

After us came the McGargles, who sneaked through the broken rocks on either side of the Gate without a single disaster, for the fallen Gate no longer sparked. Then they pushed forward and led us through the long, twisting tunnels till we came at last out into a meadow at the far end of the Wooing Path.

Blinking in the unexpected light and breathing the fresh air gratefully, we turned and said our farewells to our hairy friends, who seemed somewhat uncomfortable in the sun.

"We'll come and shear you once a year," I promised, making a cutting motion with my pointer finger and long finger. "It'll be lots faster than your trees."

Gargle translated for me, and after he was done, all of the trolls gurgled and whooped, and the littlest one hugged me, with that rough rumbly sound in its throat. Then they all turned and disappeared back into the tunnels.

"I wonder if they'll eat more than fish now," I said. "And bats."

"And mushrooms," Dusty added.

I shuddered. I never did like mushrooms, thick slimy things.

"What is wrong with mushrooms?" asked Grey.

There would be plenty of time to tell him.

Dusty and young Grey and I walked quickly the rest of the way home, trailing rock dust, guano dust, and a bit of still-swirling vortex that made us look like small whirling dervishes. I'd read about dervishes in the *D* section of the library. There was no flying. Carrying the two of us along would have exhausted Dusty, and I needed him healthy and whole.

Grey had to stop every once in a while to hitch up his trailing trews.

Finally, after about the fifth stop, I said, "Where's that knife of yours?"

"Knife?"

"Try your boot," Dusty said.

Grey reached into his boot and brought out the knife. I took it from him and trimmed the bottoms of his trews, and after that, we had no trouble racing down the path.

In a few minutes, we'd reached the stand of white birches, and I pointed to the slight rise where our pavilion sat. For the first time I noticed how run-down it looked, how in need of some paint on the columns, some scrubbing on the steps.

"What is this?" Grey asked.

"Our house," Dusty said.

"Home," I said.

"It doesn't look like a house," Grey said, head cocked to one side. "Though it *does* look like a home."

We went inside, but nobody was there, and when we ran around checking in all the whimsies, reposes, follies, and belvederes, no one was there either.

"Do you suppose," Dusty said, "they're all at the castle, giving out gifts?"

I looked at the swirl of dust still playing about our feet. "Maybe we went back in time, too."

Neither one of us wanted to think of the alternative, that the entire Family but us had burst into a thousand stars.

"*We* are still here, Dusty," I finally said in the most sensible voice I could muster. "So *they* must be alive, too."

Despite my fears of how hard it would be on Dusty, we three took to the sky. Grey's wings stretched and strained, but held. It was as if he willed them to work. So hand in hand in hand, we headed toward the castle.

Even flying, it was a long way, because Dusty and Grey had to haul me along the sky road. Besides, we had to keep an eye on Grey, in case his wings suddenly collapsed, dragging the three of us down. The fresh air racing through me cleansed me of the last of the cave stuff, and for the first time in days, my head didn't hurt at all.

Once we got to the castle, we left Grey to wait outside the castle wall, on the back side where no one would see him.

"We don't want the king to know there's a new fey in his kingdom," I told him, "else he'll be expecting a present from you and"—I wasn't sure of it but said it anyway—"you might end up tied to the land as well."

That, of course, needed a longer explanation, but Dusty was clearing his throat and saying things like, "Time, Gorse." And "We have to *go,* Gorse." And finally, his voice rising to a near Shout, he declared, "Now!"

"I'll tell you about it later," I promised Grey. "Just wait."

We left him sitting under a huge oak, went around to the front side of the castle, and in through the yett. The guards recognized us immediately as Shouting Fey—the wings gave us away.

"You two are late," one burly guard told us. "Himself won't be pleased."

"He'll like our presents, though," Dusty told him. They laughed appreciatively, and passed us through.

The castle yett was as unlike the magick Gate as could be, for it was a small, dark, iron thing that could be raised and lowered from inside the castle, and was great for repelling human intruders. And the fey! Though I was not sure they knew that. For the first time in hours, my head began to throb.

So much for feeling well again, I thought.

Dusty said, "Come on, Gorse, don't dawdle. Standing under iron makes me itch."

I wasn't dawdling. I'd just realized that the Cloak was tingling a bit, which probably meant it was working again. "You go ahead," I said. "I want to catch my breath, smooth down my skirt, clean the dirt off my hands and face, and fix my hair."

"Girls!" He let out an exaggerated groan, but dutifully went on without me.

I swung the Cloak over my head and shoulders. It would feel good to be invisible after all I'd been through. Nobody looking at me, threatening me, feeling sorry for me, wanting something from me. If I could just *stay* invisible till right before I gave my gift to the baby princess, so much the better. And maybe I could get rid of the headache that had started again under the iron yett.

Invisible, I passed by the first set of guards, and then the next without their even noticing the way the air shifted. That made me smile.

When I found my way to the throne room, the king and queen were sitting on their high gilded chairs. Self-indulgence had thickened the king's neck and waist in the past year, and the strong chin that had marked generations of his family repeated itself twice more. On the other hand, the queen had become lean and exhausted, the skin stretched tightly over her cheekbones, and was marked with lines like a plotter's map. Caring for *that* baby, even with all the nurses and handmaids around, had clearly not been an easy job.

Before them was a canopied cradle, its silken draperies drawn back to reveal baby Talia, who, at present, screeched in a high-pitched voice that was demonstrating considerable staying power.

Dusty had already told Father that I was in the castle, and Mother had relayed the message to Great-aunt Gilda, who evidently had just spoken to the king.

"Then let the gift-giving commence with all appropriate speed," said the king, who never used one word where three would do. "We should have been done with all this folderol and rigmarole long before now. I was planning on going hunting today with horse and hounds, and the light is already beginning to fade. If this doesn't go as planned, I expect to see the consequences of Oath-breaking. All those stars—it should be a lovely sight." He laughed, and it wasn't a pretty sound.

So Great-aunt Gilda quickly offered beauty and placed a thornless rose by the baby's head. The baby, with one tiny fist, quickly demolished it.

In birth succession, the Aunts gifted the child with bright eyes, a perky nose, good teeth, strong legs, and small feet. Aunt Goldie, who went second to last of the Aunts, probably meant to give the child a lovely voice, but said "loud" instead. I like to think it was a mistake, but the gleam in her eye as she said it argued against that.

As she explained to the king, "A ruler *needs* a strong voice, your majesty." And he nodded at that, though the queen—who'd already been up too many nights with her squalling child—didn't look so beguiled.

My mother, for her own reasons, chose to sit out that round. And then it was the cousins' turns, and last of all, my brothers' and sisters'. By the time they were done, the princess was so overloaded with contrasting and inconsistent virtues—like quickness and patience—that she'd probably be driven mad by her tenth birthday. Or so we could hope.

Still invisible, I stood watching it all. I think Father suspected something because he kept staring at me, though I knew he couldn't actually *see* me. Elves are far more sensitive than regular fey to such things.

And then Dusty gifted the princess a good constitution, and it should have been my turn, only of course I was invisible and nobody knew I was there.

"Where *is* she?" Mother hissed at Father.

He looked around, then nodded in my general direction, for—with a *fizzzz*ing sound—the Cloak failed once again, revealing me before I had time to run my fingers through my hair or straighten my one good wing or paste a smile across my face. Evidently I also had two bright spots of fever back on my cheeks, guano and stone dust in my hair, my eyes were wild, and the tattered cloth over my head and shoulders looked ridiculous.

Solange glared at me. She was *not* happy with what I'd done to her dress. She pinched her nose with her right hand and mouthed, "You smell."

"Who *is* this ragamuffin?" said the queen. "And what is that thing on her head? No one comes into Our Presence veiled."

"Guards!" roared the king.

Father put a hand up that stopped the guards in their tracks, then turned to the king. "This is my youngest daughter, your majesty. The thirteenth fey. She has come from a sickbed to be here for Princess Talia's christening, wrapped up in her Great-grandmother's Cloak, for warmth, I suspect. Don't you think it is marvelous that she should make such an effort?"

That's not the only place I've come from, Father, I thought, stepping forward.

All that Father had just said, true as it was or as he thought it was, should have been enough to stop anything bad happening from then on. But of course, there was still accident-prone me, stumbling toward the cradle, the spindle thrust out before me. Without realizing what I was doing, I stepped on one of the cradle's rockers, and the whole thing began to tilt back and forth precariously.

The queen screamed. The king roared again.

Providentially, her attention caught by the movement, the baby stopped crying. Her parents were stunned into silence by the miracle of it.

Into that sudden silence, I croaked, "For Princess Talia—

a present of Life." And I pulled on the thread wrapped around the spindle. However, it turned out to be the very thread that Orybon had snapped. He must have rewrapped it around the spindle—in a fit of tidying up or as a bad joke. I was never to know which.

I looked at the short thread in horror.

Everyone in the court gasped, and the queen cried out, "Not Life but Death."

The king roared and thundered, "Seize her!"

The guards rushed forward again.

But at that moment, the blessed Cloak *fizzzz*ed again, and I disappeared. I took several steps back, then dropped the spindle and thread, which became visible once they left my hand. Turning quickly—and still invisible—I headed for the door.

However, Father knew where I was the whole time, though he never told any of the Family, not even Mother, afraid that one of them might give me away, if only by a sideways glance. Instead, he bent down and picked up the spindle and thread and shook his head. Sniffed the thread. Shook his head again. All this sniffing and shaking distracted the king and queen and guards, and they stopped looking for me.

I stood silent and invisible at the door to watch what was to happen.

"What damage?" whispered Mother. Or at least she meant to whisper. It came out, as did everything the Family says in fear or haste, as a Shout. The walls of the throne room echoed with it. But since she hadn't made a Wish at the same time, at least there was no actual breakage.

"Indeed," asked the king, in a voice that promised difficult times ahead. "What damage?"

Father took out his spectacles—he only uses them for measuring, not reading—plus a measuring stick and a slide rule, the last being something he'd put together long ago from instructions he found in a manual from the future. He measured out the piece of thread. After a moment, he shook his head. "By my calculations, fifteen years, give or take a month."

The king knew this was so because Father was an elf, and everyone knew about elves being Cursed into telling the truth.

The queen burst into a torrent of tears, and the king clutched his hands to his heart and fell back into his chair. Talia started crying again, but Solange surreptitiously rocked the cradle with her foot and that quieted the baby at once.

"*Do* something!" the king commanded. "I Bid you do something *now*!"

And as it was a Bidding, Mother had to obey.

"Luckily," she said, her voice purposely silky, "I have not yet given my gift, sire, so I propose to do that now."

I'd never heard her use that voice, and it made me suddenly suspicious. Mother must have guessed that I might mess up my gift-giving, and she'd just made a prudent decision to wait till after I, as the last of the children, offered my present. The *right* decision, as it turned out.

Father cleared his throat, a sure sign that he was letting her know *he* didn't believe in that kind of luck, even though the king might.

Mother ignored him and continued. "My gift was to have been a happy marriage, but this must take precedence, of course."

"Of course, of course," said the king, waving his hand impatiently. "If the child is dead at fifteen, what use would a happy marriage be?"

At this, the queen's sobs increased to such a pitch, I thought she might actually have some Shouting Fey in her.

So Mother took the spindle and the forlorn bit of broken thread from Father. I bit my lip and tried to think of Grey outside, lonely and puzzled, but it was no good. I was fixated on the scene before me.

There was Mother, holding the thread in her right hand, the spindle under her left arm. With a quick movement of her fingers, she tied the thread back to its broken mate, knotting it securely. Then she mumbled a spell, which was really just a recipe for quick-rise bread. Everyone in the Family knew this, and there were suppressed smiles and held breath all around.

But the royals and the other guests and the guards were oblivious to what she was actually saying, since the spell was said in the Old Fey tongue and sounded rather grand and promising.

Meanwhile, Mother carefully unwound the now much-longer piece of thread. Next she measured it slowly with a calculating eye. Finally, she bit through the thread with a loud, satisfying *snick*.

"There," she told the king, the queen being too busy sobbing to hear. "Talia shall have a long, long life now. But . . ."

"But what?" the king asked.

Between sobs, the queen heard the king, and echoed him. "But what?"

"But there is still this rather worrying large knot at her fifteenth year."

The king shouted at her, "Get on with it. Get on with it." Angry spit spattered from his mouth. He waved his hands about. "You fey are really the most exasperating lot. Say it plainly. Make a spell. Do not let my child suffer. And, you nurses, get her to sleep. And, you fey, none of your riddles. Make it simple. Make it fast."

Mother was almost ready to Shout back at the king, which would have been disastrous in the extreme, when Father elbowed her, and not at all gently. Swallowing hastily, Mother said, "As you will, majesty. This knot means that instead of dying, Talia shall fall asleep on her fifteenth birthday."

"Give or take a month," Father inserted.

"And she will sleep *for as long as it takes* for this knot to be unraveled." Mother smiled at him in a very strange way. Any one of the Family would have immediately distrusted her, but not the king. I tried to figure out what she was doing, and failed.

"And, your majesty," Mother continued, "as she should not sleep without companions, nor would you want to be without her all that time, you and all in her castle shall sleep with her."

The king looked relieved. "Sleeping is so much better than dying. That's a good spell. Make it so."

The queen smiled, smoothing out many of her worst wrinkles but adding several new ones around her mouth. "Oh, that should take *no* time at all."

Mother smiled back—*she* had no wrinkles—and said nothing. The queen was not the one who was doing the Bidding, so the smile never reached Mother's eyes.

However, Father, ever honest, opened his mouth to explain what was about to happen, and Mother elbowed him in the side. He swallowed hastily, and this time, *he* was the one to shut his mouth.

Lies take spoken words, at least according to the strictures of his family Curse.

Just then I became visible again, but at that point, no one really cared.

· 17 ·

ADOPTION

I left them to their arguments and goodbyes, and went outside to find Grey. He was lying on his stomach, watching ants run up and down a blade of grass.

I sat down next to him and told him a shortened version of the story of his life in the cave as best I remembered.

He listened quietly, then said, "I remember Prince Orybon. He seems nice." He bit his lip. *"Seemed?"*

I said, "Tenses are hard."

He laughed. "Memories harder."

I laughed with him. "We are going to be *great* friends, both now and in the future."

"I'd like that," he said to the ants, his cheeks reddening. "Especially the part about actually *having* a future."

We watched the ants run in and out of their hole for as long as it took for the Family to leave the castle, and then we went home with them. By the time we got back to the pavilion—walking not flying, because we were all much too exhausted from the christening to chance the air—we'd adopted Grey.

Or rather Great-aunt Gilda adopted him. After all, he was the only one of us who had known her Mother and Father, Fergus and Maeve, having been part of the Unseelie world as they courted and were Cursed.

"I'd always wondered what happened to that scoundrel Orybon," Great-aunt Gilda said to Grey. "Mother and Father didn't know, of course."

So then I had to give her all the details of how I'd met both Orybon and Grey. Great-aunt Gilda listened with special concentration when I got to the Shouting parts and how I thought I'd killed Gargle. At that point, I burst into tears, and Grey tried to comfort me.

"I'm not crying because I'm sad, Grey," I told him. "But because I'm happy."

He looked puzzled at that. I suppose boys are often puzzled by girls. Great-aunt Gilda just looked amused.

So I explained about the cave trolls and how I'd merely given Gargle a permanent shave with my Shout.

"I suppose it's time to teach you Shouting Proper," Great-aunt Gilda said. "With your obvious talents, it's past time, actually." Then she sighed deeply. "Though from the sound of it, there are some parts you'll have to teach me as well."

Father mounted an expedition through the caves with the older boys, to seek out the Unseelie Court. They came upon a passage on the far side of the fallen Gate that led down and down into deeper, darker passages where at last they found a few of the older fey men who still dwelt there in be-glamoured splendor.

The old ones seemed a bit puzzled by the explorers. When questioned, none of them even remembered the names of Orybon and Fergus, much less their parents.

Father tried to persuade them to return above ground with him and the boys, to live with us in their own whimsies and belvederes, but they were horrified at the suggestion and too set in their ways to even come for a visit.

"How far they have fallen," Father said on his return. "They spend their days chewing on the ends of their mustaches, which have grown seven or eight feet long. And their nights quarreling over who said what to whom."

"But the stories, Father . . ." Dusty urged. "Tell them about the stories."

Father shook his head and looked sad. "They recount adventures that sound like little more than the tales children tell, not real at all. It was sad."

"Sad," Necrops and Carnell echoed.

Dusty looked down at his feet. "I *liked* the stories," he said.

"I did, too," Grey told him, putting a comforting hand on his shoulder. But later he'd confided in me, "I didn't recognize anyone there. They didn't recognize me."

Great-aunt Gilda sent down fresh apples in season to tempt them, but they lived on in the dark cave, eating only glamoured mushrooms, which they clearly preferred. After one or two more attempts, we left them alone. I think *we* became part of their stories as they had become part of ours.

"Perhaps it is easier that way," Grey said to me. "Less agony all around."

I wasn't convinced, and said so. It was one of the only times we argued.

Oddly, Mother had looked pleased at the old feys' response. "We've been lucky in our exile."

"Even with the Biddings?" I asked, astonished.

She nodded. "Even with."

As for Grey, he fit right in with the boys, playing mumblety-peg and sneaking squibs in the tree house. He was very good at both. Dusty and he became all but inseparable. The times they weren't together, Grey was in the library with Father and me. He was especially fond of mechanics and read lots of manuals that Father let him borrow. Once he made a thing called a Self-Driving Mobile Cart that ran on magick rather than being pulled by horses.

"Though," he said, "in the future, according to this book"—and he showed me a copy of a book called *Wheels for the World: Henry Ford, His Company, and a Century of Progress*—"there will be many such carts and they will run on horsepower without the actual steeds."

"How is that possible?" I asked.

"With something called 'gas,'" he said, shaking his head. "I'm not quite sure how it's done. At least not yet. Gas"—he grinned—"and oil."

"Like the oyl in the cave?" I leaned over his shoulder, and he showed me where it was written, spelled in a way that I thought positively stupid.

"Possibly," he said. "Though, again, I'm not yet quite sure how."

Later on, he made a better model of the Self-Driving Mobile Cart and hauled it to the end of the Wooing Path loaded with kitchen utensils, where he gave the whole thing to the McGargles. I went with him, and there was a lot of hooting and dancing. I brought along my silver shears and cut everyone's hair. Excepting Gargle's, of course. His fire-cut never grew back.

Grey and I also read lots of poetry together and faerie tales, and when we grew up . . . well, that's another story.

•

But we did grow. Fourteen human years went by, though it was more like a half dozen months in fey time.

Princess Talia, she of the bright eyes, perky nose, good teeth, strong legs, small feet, and extremely loud voice, spent those fourteen years as though she'd an eternity to enjoy herself, learning little but how far the bad temper she'd inherited from her father could take her. The other gifts we'd given her—wit and patience and quickness—she spent prodigally with the bad company she kept. She was always short on gratitude, kindness, and love, which take rather longer to bestow than a morning's christening. Besides, those attributes hadn't been on our list, since no royal father ever thinks to ask for such things.

I spent much of the fourteen human years—when not with Grey—reading through the *L* section of the library. Since there wasn't a lot in *I–J–K* except stuff about Indians, meaning the first people in the realm of America and Indians from India—which confused me at first—and, in *J*, the planet Jupiter and jam making, which I tried with Aunt Glade in her kitchen, where we made a mess, and I ate so much, my stomach hurt after for two days. Oh, and a place called Japan, where people slept on mats on the floor and huge men wrestled in rings to the delight of the onlookers. As for *K*, most of the books we had were about katydids and building kitchens, neither subjects of any interest to me.

But the *L* books were legion. I discovered I had an aptitude for Logic, which surprised everyone but Father and Grey. I also studied Liturgy, Lepidoptery, and Linguistics, which meant I could do spells that involved butterflies in fifteen different dialects. It was rarely useful but always pretty.

Solange questioned my accomplishments and Grey's as well. "If we can never leave this land, why do we need motor carts or more than one language?"

We tried to explain love of learning to her, but it was like trying to explain paint colors to a wall.

Father showed up in the middle of our argument and tried to mediate. At last he said, "Remember, when fifteen human years are up—"

"Give or take a month," I added.

"—things may be very different around here." He wouldn't elaborate.

I discussed this later with Grey. We were sitting in the meadow, covered by the Cloak of Invisibility so no one would disturb us.

"*How* different do you think Father means?" I asked.

He shrugged, his eyes full of wondering. "It will be a lot quieter with the princess asleep?" he ventured. "Fewer Biddings."

In the time since he'd been adopted, there had been Biddings that involved a small war to the east of the kingdom, two lords falling in love with the same young woman, and seven different demands that we spin straw into gold after the queen read a book of faerie tales to her daughter. It was Aunt Gardenia who managed it, but of course, being fey gold, it disappeared back to straw by the next morning. The queen was furious, but the king just laughed and said, "You should have spent it at once instead of staying up all night counting, my dear." Of course, Aunt Gardenia had to make herself scarce for two months, until the queen got over her dangerous grump.

There was also a Bidding of such stupendous stupidity from Princess Talia about building a bathing pool in the throne room: it ended up flooding out two sessions of the king's meetings with his advisers. After that, the king Bid us not to take any more Biddings from Talia until she'd grown into her majority or moved into a place of her own.

On her fifteenth birthday—her majority—Talia Bid all the local fey to come to her party, with the exception of me. Nobody wanted me around, tripping over the royals and possibly killing someone with an accidental Shout. I'd been left off of every guest list since the princess's christening, as had Grey, since he wasn't officially on the kingdom's birth rolls to begin with. In fact, outside of the Family, no one knew he was here. I made sure of that with a silencing spell, so no one—especially not Cambria, Arian, or Thorn—could by mistake tell a human, for as everyone knows, humans can never actually keep secrets.

My sisters and brothers and cousins were all jealous that we didn't have to go, but there was nothing they could do about it.

Grey and I planned to spend the party time in the library, drinking lavender-laced dew from Great-grandmother Banshee's crystal goblets and reading poetry to each other. At midnight Father promised he would read us ghost stories by the fire, because Grey had conceived a passion for a writer called M. R. James. It was Father's present to Grey because this day was not only Talia's birthday, but in a way it was Grey's birthday, too, for in just a few days, it would be fifteen years since he'd come to the Family. Of course, he was only about sixteen in fey terms.

Though we were having a quiet time, Talia was not. She'd invited all the neighboring royals and toffs to her party, which she called a "Sleepover Ball." The invitations said that everyone was to come in nightclothes. She herself had ordered a special new gown for the occasion that resembled a *peignoir,* which is a very grown-up nightgown with peekaboo lace and little pink ribbons sewn in strategic places. I'd read about such things years ago in a softbound book called *The Bedtime Boutique* in the *B* section. Silly things, I thought then, and still do.

Great-aunt Gilda had said that under no conditions could any of the Family go in such costumes, except Solange managed to turn one of her old nightgowns into something that was so pretty and at the same time so unrevealing that Mother let her go in that.

Now, Princess Talia was very precocious in some ways and absolutely thick in others, and she had a genius for a kind of innocent-seeming seduction. There was not a male member of the royalty for hundreds of miles around who was not pining after her, as well as several fowlers, the two stable boys, and the pig keeper, all languishing for love of her.

Even Dusty, who at eighteen usually had rather common tastes, was smitten with her and planned to go to the party with a handful of crushed basil in each pocket as an aid to making her fall in love with him. Father absolutely forbade any love potions or spells. The twins sneakily substituted pepper grains, and Dusty spent much of the early evening snuffling and sneezing into a handkerchief coated with the tiny black specks till the princess Bid him go home at once, which almost broke his heart.

Father would never have been invited because elves simply don't party, and Mother and all the Aunts were allowed to beg off, as this was an event just for the young folk.

Grey and I had watched from the pavilion steps along with Mother and Father as my twelve siblings and ten cousins flew into the moonlight, the wind feathering their wings. As usual, Cousin Alliford was trailing the pack. Granta had clumsily let her legs droop instead of keeping them straight behind, toes pointed like a rudder, so she was flying wobbly. Whey-faced and whiny, Mallow kept yelling at the others not to go so fast. Maribel, who'd recently had a conversion to vegetarianism, had tucked a bag of edibles in her pocket because she knew the royals served mostly piles of bloody butchered meats at their parties and she would have starved otherwise. And sweet Arian flew loop-de-loops like an angel yet still managed to keep up, smiling all the while.

As they passed the moon, like dust motes through light, I had a sudden memory of the thousand stars over the Gate when Orybon had burst, and began to shiver. Grey put his arm around me, and Father went into the pavilion for one of Mother's shawls. Mother patted my hand and said, "There! There!"

They thought it was simply the cold. Or that I was sad not to be going to the party. But it was not. "The fifteenth year, give or take a month," I whispered, my voice further thinned out by the night air.

Father and Mother exchanged a glance. They held hands, then reached out for my hand. I reached out for Grey's.

We closed our eyes and spoke the spell.

Far frae earth and far frae barrows,
Up to where the blue sky narrows . . .

Grey kept up. He'd always been a quick learner and never forgot a spell once he heard it.

Wind and wildness, wings and weather,
Allie-allie up together.
Now!

The *Now* called out all the Aunts from their houses, and Mother said—in a voice that carried but was not quite a Shout—"It's time for the Princess Talia spell."

None of them asked Mother how she knew.

As we all lifted into the air—Mother on one side of Father, who had no wings, and Grey on the other—I could already feel the beginnings of a magick headache coming on, and my shoulders started to hurt as well from holding them stiff against the headache pain. I relied more on the others as we barreled through the air, just as I had all those human years ago with my sprained wing.

Halfway through the journey, we met Dusty flying back the other way.

"Come with us," Father said.

"Where?"

"To the castle."

"But the princess sent me home."

Father laughed. "And *we* are bringing you back."

A slow smile spread over Dusty's face. Clearly, he'd already begun to forget about the princess and was thinking of another girl. He'd mentioned a dairy maid to me.

I said, "There's magick to be made and a spell to be finished. And with the princess asleep, there will be no thousand stars bursting."

That made him even happier.

By the time we landed at the palace, we knew we were late. The sleeping spell had already begun. There was a cook asleep with her hand raised to strike the scullery maid, and she, poor little wench, had been struck by sleep instead. It had happened at the moment of her only retaliation against the cook, which she got by kicking the cook's cat. The cat, unaware of the approaching kick, was already snoring with one paw wrapped around a half-dead sleeping mouse.

Along the hallways guards slept at their posts. One had been caught in the act of cleaning his teeth with the point of his rather blunt knife, one was peeling an orange with his sword, one was scraping his boot with his javelin tip, and one was unceremoniously picking his nose.

Dressed in nightgowns and nightshirts, the partiers snored and shivered and twitched but did not wake. And in the midst of them all, lying in state, was Talia, presents piled at her feet. She blew delicate little bubbles between her partially opened lips, and under her closed eyelids, I could see the rapid scuttling of dreams.

Being immune to the spell, my siblings and cousins hovered nervously around the tableaux, and Solange fluttered above. Dusty darted in three times to steal a kiss from the sleeping Talia. But—as he admitted later—she was so unresponsive, he tired of the game.

"I'm not a necrophile, after all," he said petulantly.

Laughing, Grey said, "Cousin, that's a funny thing to say, since only last week you were in love with the ghost of a dairy maid buried near Miller's Cross."

"He neglected to say it was a *dead* dairy maid," I said.

"That's different," Dusty countered.

"Really, Dusty?" I asked pointedly, but he refused to look at all embarrassed.

Mother put her fingers to her mouth and whistled everyone to her. "Check every corner of the castle," she told us. "I need to know for certain that every human here is asleep. And if not, why not. Meet on the staircase when you are done."

And away they all flew, except for me. I stuck close

to Father, my head now throbbing too badly to fly about. Mother's whistle hadn't helped, either. But the rest of the Family went all through the king's castle checking every room, including the garderobe.

There were sleepers in every one.

We met on the sweeping castle stairs, and Father announced, "Time for a Family conference." He led us out of the castle by the huge steps that ran down into the formal gardens, past the sleeping guards at the gate.

"Do you all understand what's happened?" Mother asked.

Necrops raised his hand. "Gorse's spell worked."

The rest all nodded, and some said my name aloud. I shuddered.

Mallow, of course, complained. "You could at least have waited till the party was over. We *never* get to go to parties."

"Don't be an idiot. We've been to Talia's birthday parties every year," Thorn said. "And they've all been dreadful, because we're not invited to them, but merely Bidden!"

They started squabbling about it, until Willow said, "Why are we quarreling amongst ourselves? We should make Gorse—"

Grey interrupted her. "It may be Gorse's *spell*," he said, "but that does not mean it is Gorse's *fault*."

"Actually," said Mother, "the sleeping part of the spell is *mine.* And they are going to sleep for a hundred years."

Everyone gasped at that, and after—for a moment—they hushed. It was one thing to want to blame me for the whole mess, but no one dared blame Mother.

"Why a hundred years?" Grey asked, and Necrops explained.

"That's the longest amount of time any spell is allowed to last." He turned to Mother. "Right?"

She nodded. *"And* you're forgetting the most important thing," she reminded them.

They looked at one another and, not seeing that *most important thing* written on anyone's face, turned to Mother, and said in chorus, "What?"

Only Grey and I were silent because we had both guessed what she meant. We'd discussed it often as we sat in the meadow, he reading poetry aloud to me as I plaited daisies into chains. Mother had confirmed it as we'd flown to the castle.

"The knot in the thread, children, you must remember the knot." She shook her head as if she'd found them all wanting. And I suppose she had.

Father held a finger up. "The Laws of Correspondence and Balance . . . ?" he prompted.

The Aunts looked at one child after another, waiting for the answer.

I couldn't stand the silence a moment longer. "Father means, of course, that to balance such an important spell, a similar knot must be set around the castle."

"Ohhhhhhh." It was a communal sigh.

Grey reached out and held my hand. Dusty grabbed his other hand. The rest all situated themselves in a great circle and held the hands of the person on either side. Only I at one end, and Mother where we would have touched hands, did not complete the circle. Instead, we each waved our free hand widdershins.

A great wind began to blow from the north. It plucked out the pepper seeds from Dusty's pockets, and picked the seeds from the queen's thorn that stood in the raised center of a grand fountain. The wind gathered rose hips and acorns and flung them into the air. Faster and faster the maelstrom blew, a great black tunnel of air that was like and unlike the vortex that had whirled away the years of Grey's exile.

In a voice as wild as the wind, Mother said, "A hundred times, children. One for each year the princess and her court shall sleep."

And then she and I spoke the spell, for she'd taught it to me as we'd sped through the skies to the castle:

Blow and sow
This fertile ground

Until the knot
Be all unwound.

It was spare, and perfect. *Some day*, I thought, *I want to be able to make spells as compact and perfect as that. Though it's probably not a learned thing, but a gift.*

On the second round, Father and Grey and Dusty spoke the words as well. On the third, the rest of the Family joined in, though Arian managed only the rhyme word at the end of the second and fourth line. But then, it didn't matter. The spell was wound up even without him.

By the time we had reached the seventies, my head felt as if someone had split it with an iron bar. In the eighties, I was nauseated. By the nineties, I was shaking like aspen leaves in a puzzling wind.

Before we actually reached one hundred, I'd stopped speaking the spell aloud and just whispered the words.

Mother ended the spell with the loudest Shout I'd ever heard her make. It was so loud, the earth itself was shocked and opened up dozens and dozens of little mouths. Into every one of those tiny mouths popped a seed or rose hip or nut and, in moments, they began to grow. We watched as the growing years were compressed into seconds, green shoots leaping upward toward the sky.

By the time the last echo of Mother's Shout had died away, a great forest of mammoth oaks and thorny vines, rosy briars and pepper trees surrounded the palace. Only one small passage overhead remained open, where the moon beamed down a narrow light. Inside the rest of the knotted wood, it was as dark as a dream, as deep as a hundred-year sleep.

"Come, children," Father said.

We rode the moonbeam up and out, Mother dragging Father, and Grey carrying me, for I was almost as comatose as the inhabitants of the castle, felled by the amount of magick around me.

As the last of us—Arian, of course—passed through the hole, the thorns sewed themselves shut over the deathlike silence.

·18·

AND AFTER

"Will a hundred years be enough?" I asked Mother the next day when she brought me a tisane for my headache and was fussing around my bed.

"It was the most I was allowed," she said.

"I know that." I drank a bit of the tisane. It was elderberry, my favorite. "But near the end, couldn't we go and knot the spell anew?"

"Really, Gorse, it's all that's needed," she said, shaking her head at me. And out she went.

I was still puzzling this when Grey came in with a book from the *H*'s—History.

"This looks like something that might interest you," he said.

The book was about the rise of a religion called Democracy, which believes in neither monarchs nor magick. He read it to me all day and in the evening he came to a passage about how "Democracy encourages the common man."

"Nothing common about you," I told him.

"Nor you," he said.

"I'm not a man," I said, a little more loudly than I'd meant to.

"I've noticed," he said in the sweetest way, startling me. He put down the book then and we just looked at one another for a long while.

Afterward, Father and Mother explained to Grey and me that the hundred years was the amount of time the kingdom had to remain without a king of the royal blood ruling over it before the kingdom could legally be declared no longer his.

"I finally found it about a month ago," Father said. "All along, it was in one of the books that Great-aunt Gilda had from her Mother, a piece of paper signed by King Carmody sewn into the book's lining. It's all about how a king or his family must rule the land for a hundred years with his immediate line continuing after him. Your Mother called me brilliant, and I guess I am." He chuckled.

"He is," said Mother, gazing at him with the kind of love I'd always missed seeing. "No one else in the Family could have figured it out. It's why I put the hundred years in the spell."

"And that means what?" asked Grey.

"Ah," said Father, raising his finger, which is how he signals that he has come to the point of a story.

But I understood before he had time to say another word. "If the king no longer owns the kingdom or the land," I explained to Grey, "he no longer owns *us*." I looked at Father. "Am I right?"

"*You* are the brilliant one," Father said, nodding.

"Then all the ties will be severed!" I stood up and danced around the room.

Grey stood up and danced with me for a moment, but suddenly stopped mid-step. "But what if in a hundred years a prince comes, gets in through the briar hedge, and marries the princess?"

Mother looked at Father, and Father looked down at the floor.

"Wait!" I cried. "Wait! Grey has already found the solution."

He looked stunned. "I have?"

That was when I showed them the passage in the Democracy book about the rise of the common man.

"Interesting," said Father.

"I don't see why," Mother said. "We aren't common—we're fey."

I sat up in bed. "Really, Mother, think!" I didn't realize how much I was sounding like Father then, but now Grey was doing the chuckling. "In a hundred years, even if some enterprising young prince manages to arrive just as the knot of the briary wood is unraveling, I shall be there, in the Cloak of Invisibility. Even if he decides to marry her without her money and her kingdom, he will be too late to tie us to the land. Besides, I will whisper the Rote of Revolution in his ear. And if the Cloak works long enough, Talia will seem to him only a musty relic of a bygone era, with a voice like a saw cutting wood. Her bedclothes will reek of decadence and her bubbly breath of decay. He will wed the scullery maid out of compassion and learn . . ." I tried to think of what he would learn.

"Computer science," Grey said.

"What's that?"

"Something very complicated and magickal," he said. "Just the sort of thing I like."

I nodded. "Computer science it is. The only Biddings we shall ever have to answer to from now on will be our own.

And we shall be allowed to travel outside the kingdom's borders." I was thinking of the Great Wall of China, of the iced mountains of the Antarctic, of the Hanging Gardens of Babylon.

Mother laughed at me as if she'd read my thoughts. "You have such odd longings, child. I am so glad you will get your Wishes."

"And you, too, my darling," Father said, his hand on her arm. "Though I always hoped, I never dared to truly believe it would happen."

I was stunned by his admission but said nothing about it directly. I told him instead, "Sometimes freedom is simply won by a long patience, something that works far better than any magick spell."

"And it's all because of you, my darling daughter," Father said. "Who came into the castle veiled by the Cloak. Who reappeared out of a deep dark space and liberated the ancient troll race. Who flew again on new wings to sever every bond and tie."

Mother's mouth was agape. "The prophecy."

Father nodded.

"Well," said Mother, "I always thought she might be the One!"

"I actually thought it might be Grey," I said, glancing over at him. "New wings, liberating the trolls, and all."

"No, my darling thirteenth child," said Mother, "I always *knew* you were the One, though no one else believed me!"

"She is indeed," said Grey, "the One." And the smile he gave me lit up the entire room.

But I knew what the others didn't even suspect. The magick came not from being the One, but being the Two, for One and One together—like arrows in a quiver being stronger than a single one on its own—meant that Grey and I were stronger together than apart for . . . well, for as ever after as is possible.